FIRST SIGHT

Sight, Book One

Jordan Taylor

A NineStar Press Publication

Published by NineStar Press
P.O. Box 91792,
Albuquerque, New Mexico, 87199 USA.
www.ninestarpress.com

First Sight

Printed in the USA
First Edition
May, 2018

Print ISBN: 978-1-948608-71-8

Also available in eBook, ISBN: 978-1-948608-67-1

The short story *Hindsight* was originally published under the title *Sight* as part of the anthology *Best Gay Romance 2014* – Cleis Press, 2014.

Warning: This book contains sexual content, which may only be suitable for mature readers.

Despite misgivings, newlyweds Noah and Archer set out for a dream honeymoon in Amsterdam with a shoestring budget and negligible travel experience between them. All goes well until they leave home.

Noah, who once hoped to become a comic book or graphic novel illustrator, is completely blind due to a degenerative eye disease and has rarely left the Seattle area since his diagnosis. While Archer has never previously traveled for longer than a weekend with Noah along.

Reaching the Netherlands, they face a chaotic world better suited to a particularly alert cat than a young blind man and his novice guide. If the physical fear and stresses of public transportation and city streets are not bad enough, Noah and Archer find even their marriage threatened by the daily battle they wage without and within their own relationship.

Includes a bonus story! Go back to the beginning with the prequel and see how Noah and Archer first met and how their relationship evolved.

For everyone who has ever gone traveling. And missed a step.

HINDSIGHT

ARCHER'S VOICE MINGLED with rushing waves and biting wind as he spoke into my ear. "There's a ship. State ferry, car and passenger, white and green. Seagulls catching rides in the wake."

Sunlight soaked my left side. Archer stood against my right. A mix of musty, salty, crackling odors swirled through the breeze amidst a cacophony of waves. Dead crabs, live fish, decomposing seaweed, rotting driftwood, all churned among ocean brine that haunted the nose like a brilliant flash haunts the eyes. And wet dog. Luath leaned into my left leg. Even off duty, I carried her harness and she would hardly leave my side.

"Can you get Luath to chase the birds?" I asked. "She's not having much fun."

"She won't listen to me."

"You tease her."

"The gulls moved on." Pause, Archer turned his head beside mine. "Crows on driftwood up the beach behind us. Luath, *look*, go get the birds."

I felt him fling out his arm to point for her.

Luath did not move, her warm presence shielding my legs from wind.

"Sometimes, I think she doesn't trust me," Archer said, his lips brushing my ear.

Wasn't he self-conscious on the public beach with his arm across my waist? He had always been stressed about those things. The only sounds were the waves, wind, a few birds, Luath panting by my knee—though I knew we stood not far from campsites.

"I don't blame her," I said.

"No? You trust her more than me?"

"I've learned from experience to second-guess your directions more than hers. Human errand. Nothing personal."

Another pause, only wind twisted past. Then Archer said, "You mean, human *error*?"

"That's what I said."

"You said *errand*."

"Close enough."

"What dictionary are you using?"

Luath nudged the harness in my hand. I didn't like this part—making judgments to say if my dog was better off doing the work she loved, or imposing freedom. At least she had managed some relaxation over the past two days in the San Juans.

"No criticizing on vacation," I said, opening buckles on the harness.

"Don't you mean, 'No cannibalizing on vacation'? That would be close enough."

"God, Archer, you're worse than my mother. It's not a crime to get a word wrong."

"Maybe not, unless you've swallowed a library."

I bent to harness Luath. She licked my hands, wagging her whole rear against my legs.

Archer chuckled. "Such a blonde."

"Now you're cannibalizing my dog."

"Did you really just say that?"

I stood up with the harness handle and short leather leash to her collar in my left hand.

"I'm not criticizing your dog." I heard the grin in his voice as he put his arm around me once more. Leaning into my shoulder, he kissed my ear. "I love your dog. I love you, Noah."

"Overcompensating."

"Sorry."

"Isn't the sun setting? Should we start for camp?"

"Camp?" His lips curved upward against my neck. "You mean the eight-bedroom, turreted Victorian B and B we're staying in?"

"Shall we go?"

"It's just before the show starts. The sky's blinding, golden white, then bright blue."

A car engine sounded far off. Campers packing on Sunday evening after a weekend of Pacific Northwest sand and sun. Perhaps we were within sight of other tourists after all, yet Archer remained against me, talking into my ear about colors, waves, and seabirds.

I dropped the harness handle to reach for Luath's silky head, resting my fingers across the curve of her skull.

"It's sinking," Archer said.

Good. Nearly time to go. For our last night here, maybe Archer would humor me with carryout pizza or fish and chips so we didn't have to eat in public.

"Yellow, turning orange, turning pink," Archer said. "There's another ship. Looks like it's plated in gold. The seagulls' wings are flashing flames. Every wave catches the light as it turns and falls, like a dance with a million performers."

"How about the sand?" I asked.

"Where it's wet from receding tide, it holds light like glass. Like it's been melted down in a forge."

He kissed me again, letting his lips linger on my skin so I felt his nose, chin, eyelashes, the warmth of his breath on my neck. And sudden tension in his body.

I started to turn my head. "Archer?"

"Noah...will you marry me?"

Wind stopped roaring. Waves stopped crashing. Luath stopped panting. I felt her turn, shift in the harness to look up while my muscles grew rigid as driftwood, holding my breath. Smells vanished with sounds. Void. Empty.

"*No,*" I snapped the word, not like a refusal, but an order, even a threat. I snatched Luath's harness handle and wheeled away while my words to her were barely formed. "Luath, *left. Forward.*"

We made an about-turn and started up the beach, toward the hillside Victorian a quarter of a mile away. Luath rushed across wet sand, pulling me with her faster than I would normally allow. As if we could outrun the question, leave it buried in the sand—never to be heard from again.

I FIRST MET Archer in our freshmen year of high school, after his family moved to Olympia in February. When not in class, he'd spent much of his time until summer break standing in any uninhabited nook of the grounds. No reading, talking, texting. He just stood, waiting for the bell to ring, nearly invisible.

To my regret, I can't remember details of the first moment I saw him. I do remember the first time I *looked* at him.

Archer stood in the rain, one sneaker in wood chips around a raised flowerbed, the other foot propped on the brick edge of the bed. His black hoodie drooped across his shoulders with the weight of rain, blue jeans painted navy by water, sticking to his legs like plastic wrap. He gazed at the ground, chin tipped down. Brown hair fell across his forehead, flattened, darkened and spiky from rain running through it, across his head, over his face, dripping off the pointed nose and chin in ribbons of icy water.

I had never been in love, though I'd had a crush on a teacher in junior high and would give my left arm to be Peter Parker's sidekick—comic, movie, anywhere. So I'm not sure how I knew I had fallen in love in five seconds. But I did.

That night, I started a new comic while my parents went through their customary after-dinner shouting match downstairs and Shiloh danced in her room, listening to pop music. Though Shiloh was four years younger than me, I let her help work on my comics. She had a genius for plot twists that went far beyond her years. I usually drew while she announced ideas.

This time, I closed my door, starting a new notebook of sketches that no one in my family would be allowed to see.

I can still envision that first sketch: the gray, dull light, water sliding through his hair, down his temples, perfect shape of his nose and chin, curve and angle of his body against muted school grounds, low brick wall of the dead, dirt flowerbed, and his fixed stare into nothing.

I approached Archer the next day. Confidence, like art, was a family trait. I'd hawked my mom's handmade jewelry and paintings at art fairs for as long as I could remember, argued with my sister about the colors she chose to match— pink and orange were favorites—since she was old enough to dress herself, and learned to sneer at "imitators" by the age of ten.

"Hey," I said to Archer through the crowd as he closed his locker. "Want to hang out sometime? Do you play MMOGs?"

He stared at me, hostile blue eyes sunken against dark circles. For the first time, it occurred to me that he looked like someone who hadn't had a proper night's sleep—or meal—in weeks. He seemed about to curl his lip. Instead, he walked away. Not a word.

Mouth open, I stood in the hallway like a moron while peers flowed past. Perhaps he hadn't heard properly in the commotion of the hall.

Next time I tried, later that day after lunch, I abandoned the smile. "What's your problem? Got some invisible friends here already?"

He turned from dropping a sandwich bag in the trash and directed a cold gaze at me. "Leave me alone."

Archer was an expert at cold stares, brows drawn close over blistering eyes. I couldn't get my breath, hands clenched into fists just to resist reaching for him, room whirling like a top.

His expression changed. "You all right?"

"Uh..." Still couldn't breathe properly. "I'm—ssss—"

"What?"

"Sorry to bother you."

He turned away.

"Wait!" Several people still eating looked around. "I didn't mean sorry and...done. I meant sorry and could we start over?"

"With what?" Though he glanced at me, he spoke through set teeth, as if he didn't want anyone to notice he was talking to me.

"I can't remember your name."

He stood there.

"Could you tell me?"

"Archer."

"That's a cool name."

Nothing.

"I'm Noah."

He looked at the clock on the wall over the cafeteria doors.

"Do you like comic books?" I asked.

"No."

"Movies?"

"No."

"You don't like movies?"

He shrugged. "I've got to go."

"The bell hasn't rung. Computers?"

He half glanced at me.

"We've got a new one—old one expired—and the new one's a bitch. Can't figure out half the software on it. My mom can't stand it. I'm hoping for my own laptop for my birthday, even a shoddy one, but this is what we've got now."

He looked at me.

The bell rang.

"Can you come over after school? My mom picks me up. Dinner and you can tell me how to work the desktop? If you're there, my parents won't shout at each other. We act like normal people when we have company." I beamed at him.

After a long pause, just looking at me as if I'd been speaking Swahili, Archer shrugged.

It turned out, Archer knew more about computers than Mom does about van Gogh—whose Wikipedia article she's always tweaking. He could take them apart, put them together, tell what everything did. And he programmed.

Our friendship developed along with the game we made—me drawing animation, Archer programming characters to run, jump, shoot crossbows. We didn't have much else in common. I was into art. Archer was into history. I wanted to illustrate my own graphic novels or animations. Archer wanted to travel around the world and learn new languages. But those computer games, early on, gave us all the common ground we needed.

Mom adored him—such a polite, quiet young man. Shiloh could hardly be in the same room with him, red-faced and tongue-tied.

I never "came out" to my family—which seemed lucky, though there's something to be said for an exchange of feelings. I believe my father was resigned since the day he tried to take me fishing. I had vomited in the boat at the sight of him impaling a living worm on a silver hook. Then screamed like a toddler when he got me to grab a thrashing fish that he swung aboard. I had been thirteen. He invited Shiloh after that. Shiloh loved murdering fish, then frying them herself, eating hot, greasy flesh with her fingers like a barbarian. He never mentioned taking me again.

My mother was slightly more direct, telling me, shortly after I started bringing Archer home, that she fully supported whoever I wished to be with as long as that person was positive for me. And had good taste.

Archer was far better for me than I realized at the time. I'm not sure if he had always been a brooding introvert, but he'd been handed an extra helping of brooding before he moved to Olympia. His father—a cop—was killed working a nightshift the previous summer. Archer and his mother moved from the Twin Cities to live with his grandparents until they could "get things worked out."

It would be two years before Archer said more to me about his father than he was dead. Then, only because I wished I was also dead.

It started in the fall of our junior year. We sat at the computer for a typical programming session while Mom was out fetching Thai food and Shiloh talked on the phone upstairs.

Archer typed, checking multiple screens, programming to game, sitting up straight in the desk chair as he worked on a high-jump for a humanoid cat character. I sat on a kitchen stool behind him, leaning my chin on his shoulder. We had yet to progress beyond kisses. Archer—who viewed sitting near one another in a theater or school auditorium as tantamount to a public make-out session—made it clear things were already moving plenty fast.

I blew gently in his ear to get a rise out of him.

He opened the game screen and pointed. "That what you wanted?"

"It's perfect."

"You didn't even look."

I leaned forward, my chest against his shoulder. Something blocked the screen. Like mud around the edges. I blinked, rubbed my eyes, looked again. The screen appeared normal. The catman sprang onto a platform that our human hero never could have.

"Something wrong?"

"Nothing. It's incredulous."

"What? You mean 'incredible'?"

"Awesome, perfect, rhetorical."

"Rhetorical?" He shook his head, trying not to laugh. "What was that meant to be?"

"You did a great job. Thank you." I kissed his neck.

He jumped away. Mom was unlocking the front door.

If I'd been asked, I couldn't have said what went wrong looking at the screen.

When visual glitches persisted, a vague clouding in around the edges, I kept them to myself. My parents inched closer to divorce every month. At the same time, I was in the process of getting my driver's license. If I sometimes couldn't see my sketchbook or classroom perfectly, it wasn't a big deal compared to driving and divorce.

I might have gone longer in silence if not for the driving. I picked my sister up from school one day when our mom couldn't make it. A few blocks from the crowded lot, Shiloh screamed.

"Noah! What is your problem?"

"Don't shout at me when I'm driving!"

"Don't run freaking stop signs then!"

I glanced in the side mirror. My hands shook on the wheel and I took a slow breath.

"We could've been hit," she snapped. "Or arrested."

"I'm sorry. I'm really sorry. I forgot there was one there and I didn't see it."

"It's a huge red sign, Noah."

Of course, Shiloh spilled the beans. I admitted to my mom that I'd had visual problems lately, though they hadn't seemed like such a big deal.

Driving privileges were suspended.

The next day, I stood in the optometrist's office, staring at everything. Drinking in the light through blinds making bars across the table of magazines, glossy and neatly arranged in rows. Water tank with tiny paper cups. Kid's toys: red, yellow, blue, wood and plastic. An old, battered Etch A Sketch.

There had never been so much to see. Like I grew up living inside a grocery store and only ever tried white bread and milk. Every art museum my mom ever dragged us to as kids, every school trip, every sketch and comic and movie. Every glance out the window. How could it be possible that I'd never really *thought* about sight?

You imagine they won't know. They'll send you for tests, decide treatment. Worst case, they'll cut open your eyes with lasers and you'll have recovery time ahead and photophobia.

But the doctor did know: worse, much worse than anything we'd imagined.

Retinitis pigmentosa. For some people, pretty mild. Manageable. For others, a disease that eats the eyes. And mine was already moving alarmingly fast. Incurable. Possibly leading to permanent and complete blindness within a year, or five, or ten.

At home, bewildered, shocked, with my equally lost and shocked mother, I went to bed and stared at my sketch of Archer in the rain. And stared. As if I would never get another chance.

FAR FROM NEVER seeing him again, Archer got me through the next years. That sounds churlish considering my family was also there, more or less. But I never mentioned a lot of things to them. I never told them that, by the time I was nearing eighteen—seeing only dots of the normal world in the center of my former field of vision—I'd made up my mind to kill myself. Only Archer. He took the news of my impending suicide by telling me I was a selfish, conceited ass.

"You coward," he growled, sitting on my bed one Saturday afternoon. "Do you have any idea how many tens of thousands of blind people are living and working and thriving in the world right now? Grow some, Noah. God."

I sat on the edge of the bed beside him. "You don't know what it's like—"

"I know what it's like when someone you love is dead." He spoke so fiercely, I leaned away. "What it feels like when you would kill to have him back, trade your life to bring him back. And you can't. There's *nothing* you can do. You'll excuse me for thinking you can buck up and work hard and go on living a productive life. At least no one shot you six times in the face and left you on a street corner in the middle of the night."

We sat in silence until Shiloh shouted upstairs, asking if we wanted to call for pizza.

When we stood, I finally muttered, "I won't kill myself."

"Thanks," Archer said coldly, walking out, leaving me to make my own way downstairs.

Other days, Archer lay on the floor with me, letting me run my fingertips over his lips, cheeks, jaw, eyebrows, eyelids, through his hair, across his ear, down his neck and shoulder. I turned my head, shifting my eyes to see fragments of him, memorize the blue eyes, so adept at frigid disdain. The sharp profile. The expression, not of pity or grief or anger which flooded my own family, but of determination and concentration, looking into my face.

I wasn't completely blind until well past my eighteenth birthday. Almost two years to brood, run from it, before it settled. Right about the time the divorce was finalized, Shiloh started high school, and we moved into a smaller house.

I hated that new house. Shiloh went over it with me again and again. I yelled at her when she wasn't fast enough to keep me from kicking a coffee table or knocking against a doorway because I pulled too far to the right of her guiding arm.

"Can't you watch where you're going and warn me?"

"What the hell do you think I'm trying to do?"

She stopped offering to show me around after that.

I learned Braille, took up listening to audiobooks with the frequency of an addict, finished high school a year late.

Archer started college in Seattle while interning at the same time, helping program the next generation of smartphones or tablets or antivirus software. I told him to move on, find a normal boyfriend—to which he only sighed. He did that a lot. And got a lot of extra meaning behind it compared to most people's sighs.

I sat in my room, listening to *Catch-22*, *Sense and Sensibility*, *East of Eden*, *Dracula*, *One Flew Over the Cuckoo's Nest*, *The Hobbit*...

Shiloh had me pursuing a guide dog by then. With the waiting list so long and me so young—new at this—I had low expectations. In the meantime, I listened to books, rarely leaving home except for an eye exam or other blindness-related appointment, doing sit-ups or push-ups, or only lying still inside a novel.

It took a year before my mom put her foot down and said I was acting like a child. She drove me to an agency we had visited early on. People specializing in my dilemma. They were cheerfully certain they could get me a job. They did. Unfortunately. Telemarketing for a political group of tree-huggers, thrilling my mom to death and securing me a place in her house for the time being.

The people at the agency went on about how nothing was impossible and I should continue my education. Blind people were teachers, musicians, writers, accountants, psychologists, lawyers—on and on. No reason to stay on a phone forever. No limits. So they said. Full, productive life. I just had a bad attitude.

When not making phone calls about greenhouse gas or airborne particulate matter, or using my audio email interface, I went on doing sit-ups as I listened to books, wishing Archer wasn't so painfully far away. Though I told myself he needed to stay as far from me as possible.

The new house was a two-story shack at the edge of a block of condominiums from the 1970s. A tiny park bordered the backyard beyond a dilapidated fence. When he did visit on weekends, Archer and I walked the park, or sat on a bench in the sun, saying practically nothing. No touching in public or private, other than to help me get around. I wondered if he had anyone else. Never asked.

With school out for the summer, though still working, Archer came around more. He told me what he saw as we walked or sat, or occasionally went into town together.

He never used generalities as Shiloh did: "There's a tree. Don't hit it." He used specifics: "There's a madrona just to your right. Red bark strips are peeling back in little rows like parchment curled into scrolls. The trunk underneath is soft green, smooth and clean. There's a trail of ants scurrying up a branch."

Later, I started prompting for certain things: What color were the Little League uniforms at the park's diamond? Was the groundsman using a push mower or a riding one? What kind of bird? What kind of plants?

The summer we both turned twenty, Archer rented a studio off campus and invited me over. New place. I refused, asked him over instead.

I asked how his mother was—depressed—and grandparents—glad he was doing something productive— while we shared a pizza on the couch. Like being sixteen again, no one else home, talking over our plans for the games we created.

My face felt stiff and uncomfortable. I wiped my fingers on a paper towel, reached up, and discovered I was smiling.

"What's wrong?" Archer asked, close beside me.

I shook my head. Kind of hard to explain that it had taken me by surprise to realize I felt happy.

He cleared our plates. I listened as he washed his hands in the kitchen and asked if I wanted something to drink. Footsteps, soft on carpet in the family room, then flopping back beside me.

"Don't you ever think of moving out?" He ran his fingers across the back of my neck, up through my hair.

I leaned away. "Of course. Just not much of a self-starter these days."

"Want to stay with me for a while? You could find a lot of new opportunities in the city."

"Olympia's a city." I turned my head, frowning at his voice.

He kissed me.

I pushed him away. "Stop it. Don't you meet people in school? I told you to find someone else."

"When have I ever listened to you?"

I opened my mouth, closed it, bit my lip. "That's not—"

"You could try it. I'm not about to sign you into my lease. Just try something new."

"You don't have time to be a babysitter," I muttered.

"I don't intend to be."

"I have to get to appointments and I'd be looking for another job—"

"Call a cab, get a bus, walk. You're not helpless. I'll show you around the neighborhood." He kissed me again.

I didn't push him away.

THE STUDIO TURNED out easy to navigate. His neighborhood had audio crosswalks and I'd gotten good enough with my collapsible white cane that I could get around within a few blocks of the place.

I found a customer service job with a local company growing enough that they needed phone support within business hours. Imagining I would hate it, I found that few people were really nasty on the phone and most seemed grateful when I could get them the information they needed. A tiny thing, yet it felt good to be the one doing something for someone else.

We moved into a ground-floor condo, near campus. Two bedrooms and stairs that had to be counted and mastered.

Archer was back in school. I worked, hoped to return to school and get off the phone.

Archer became a hero at home. Shiloh still had at least a borderline crush on him. Mom treated him like the second coming. Or, maybe she only treated him like he'd saved her son's life.

My dad called now and then, took me to dinner one Saturday, then asked me to his place in Olympia every other month or so after he saw that eating out was not my favorite. We never had much to say to each other—mostly about work and jobs. I hoped he was glad Archer motivated me out of the house and into a more independent future. I had to hope because we rarely mentioned Archer.

It was only a year ago, both of us twenty-two, Archer just out of school and focused on a programming career, when the news came from California about the dog.

Archer took the time off, begged his grandparents for a loan, and the two of us flew to Sacramento for the training period.

I wanted a German shepherd dog. I'd always envisioned myself walking the streets, proud and upright with a big, strong, male German shepherd in harness, ever since Shiloh first brought up the idea years ago.

But you don't choose your dog. And, I learned later, German shepherds are not so popular as service dogs these days. The wagging, licking animal introduced to me was a silky angel. Soft, smooth, smelling of lavender and dog breath, pressing her nose against my neck as I slid off my chair onto the floor on my knees.

They taught us to work together over the next weeks living at the facility. Of course, Luath already knew everything. I was the one who needed training.

Archer came and went a couple of times. Then they all arrived for graduation. Even my dad.

I hugged him, trying very hard not to cry as he whispered, "I'm proud of you, Noah."

Luath changed everything. Not just with my mobility. She changed who I was, how people saw me and interacted with me. She opened doors in so much more than a literal sense. People stopped to speak to me, offered help in the street, asked her name, her age, said how beautiful she was:

"Such a gorgeous dog—she's almost white."

"My cousin breeds white golden retrievers. Do you mind if I take a picture?"

"I bet that dog's smarter than most people. And never complains about a day's work."

Luath lived for work. And for me. And I found I had so much more to live for than I'd imagined since I was sixteen and ran a stop sign.

I had listened my way through fifteen hundred classic and modern books, nearly all in audio, a few in Braille, over the past six years. From *The Adventures of Tom Sawyer* to *War and Peace*, I'd consumed a library. And I wanted to teach about literature. I didn't know exactly how to get from where I was to where I wanted to be, but I knew a BA in English was a place to begin. I would start college this fall.

It was April when Archer suggested a long weekend away.

That morning, Luath was barking as he teased her with a ball he bounced against the wall. Sharp, demanding barks, irritated with him.

"You two are just alike," Archer said when he found me in the kitchen—Luath dashing past. She would run the ball to her bed to hide it from him.

"You're the common demeanor," I said.

"*Denominator.*" Archer shifted, sighed. I knew he had his hands on his hips.

"Don't stare at me in that tone of voice. You're the one causing trouble."

"What, pray tell, is the tone of my stare?"

"Patronizing, disbelieving, annoyed."

Luath's claws clicked on hardwood as she trotted into the room to rest her head on my knee. I sat at the kitchen table in front of my morning coffee.

"Want to go jogging with us this morning?" Archer asked.

"Are you talking to me or her? Breakfast?"

"Sure. What are you fixing?"

"I thought you might fix something."

Archer chuckled and walked away. Luath ran after him, likely to hover over her bed and the ball, making sure he didn't get any ideas.

I had scrambled eggs and toast ready when he returned. His running shoes clapped on wood. He stepped up beside me, arms around me, chin on my shoulder.

"Orange juice? Want to go away for a long weekend?"

"How?"

"I'll get a day off. They won't fire me. I was thinking the San Juans. After spring break, before summer break, sun and minimal traffic." After a pause, he added, "On me."

"Sounds great." I turned my head to kiss him.

Luath loved the big Victorian—painted pink and white outside and in, according to Archer—nosing into every corner of our room, groveling before the resident cat while off-duty. We'd never been to Washington's San Juan Islands before and Luath wasn't the only one to enjoy the change.

On Saturday night, he took me for dinner in a quiet place of other murmuring couples and a warm spot from the middle of the table where a candle burned. Much as I hated eating out, Luath, more than Archer, had taught me I wasn't the only person in this relationship.

In the back of my mind, I still waited for the day I would move on or get hit by a bus, and Archer would be free of me.

Free to have a normal boyfriend who enjoyed travel as much as he did. Free to trade in his chauffeur's license for a man he could take sightseeing without having to explain the sights.

Then, on Sunday, he stood against me at sunset, telling me about molten sand and dancing water, and asked me to marry him.

And I walked away.

Back home, I wouldn't talk about it. When Archer left for work, I packed a duffel for me, another for Luath's food, toys, brushes, then called a cab and rode all the way to Olympia with Luath across my lap.

No one home. I found the hidden key under the broken brick on the window ledge and let myself in. Luath knew the place. I removed her harness, gave her water in the kitchen, and sat on the couch until Shiloh got home.

She was about to graduate high school, tall, outgoing, with half the males in the school chasing her. She still loved art and breakup songs.

"Hello, stranger." She dropped her bag on the vintage chair with a great banging and creaking. "What are you two doing here?" She patted Luath while Luath danced about her, claws hushed on old carpet.

"Just...needed a break."

"A break? You're not here for the dazzling company? What happened?"

I shrugged. "Do you have anything to eat here? I kind of missed breakfast...and lunch."

She plunked down on the couch beside me, Luath leaping up between us. "What happened, Noah? I thought you were on a trip with Archer."

"Got back yesterday."

"And?"

I shrugged again.

"Stop it."

"I just thought I'd stay a while. If Mom doesn't mind. And there's any food."

"You want a sandwich? I was thinking about turkey on rye."

"Sure, thanks."

She stood. "Mom's going to want to know what happened."

Of course, I wasn't able to ignore them asking all through that evening.

During dinner of vegetable stir-fry on rice, I halted the conversation with, "Archer asked me to marry him. So I left."

The room went silent. No-breath silent. Then they continued eating. Not a word.

I returned to my old room. Ignored Archer's calls. Everyone else went on about their business. I worked from home, listened to books, going out with Luath because she needed the exercise, not because I wanted to go anywhere.

After two nights, Archer showed up on a workday morning. I opened the door, thinking it would be a delivery. Luath threw herself past me and I knew who stood there.

I returned to the table where my headset and laptop were set up for work.

She whined and licked while he stroked her. Then he stood at the table by me.

"When are you coming home?"

"No plans to."

"You can't go to school from here."

"I'll go somewhere else."

"Why? You already live right by the school you're set to attend."

Luath ran to me, wagging, nudging my arm, telling me with many exclamation marks that Archer had come to see us.

"Why did you only start caring about me once I was blind?" I asked.

"What?"

"You were lukewarm for years. Once I was blind, it was all, 'Won't you come live with me, Noah? Isn't this great? How about a vacation? How about getting married?' What the hell?"

"Maybe I just needed you to back off." The shock left his voice and he sounded angry. "Did you ever think of that? No. Never. Because it's all about *you*. I was shit-scared coming out to my family, okay? Not like you—just floating by. When I moved here, I had no one. No one but you and them. I wasn't about to throw one away for the other. But we grew up and you stopped being so damn pushy. Then being away from you...when I went to school—" He stopped, muscles so tense I could feel tight energy in the kitchen as he gripped the back of a chair or pushed his hand through his hair or clenched his fists.

"Being away from you was terrible. I finally had to admit to myself I loved you." His tone bristled with hostility as he went on. "It had *nothing* to do with your damn eyes... Except that it was an excuse for us to spend time together."

"I'm sorry you feel that way," I said, rigid in my chair, face turned down to the table.

"Don't be sorry. Just come home."

"So you can take care of me? Tell me if my socks are mismatched and drive me to appointments and let me know if I've missed shaving cream on my face? Be saddled with me for the rest of your life? You've made it perfectly clear how selfish you find me. This is it. You're twenty-three. You can find a normal boyfriend and not be shackled to an albatross."

"I have a normal boyfriend. Except for his pigheadedness and unconventional word choices. I've already met the person I want to be with for the rest of my life. Do you honestly think mismatched socks are a deal-breaker?"

"This is not funny, Archer."

"Isn't it? In a stupid, pointless way?"

"Go. Move on."

"Why is that your decision?"

"You asked, I said no."

"Then don't marry me, but come home anyway. This is not one-sided. You dragged me into this relationship. Now here I am. I need you no less now than when I was fifteen and sick with grief and you were the only person in the world who asked if I wanted to hang out. I want to hang out with you, Noah. Forever. Come home."

My chest hurt. My head hurt. My closed fists trembled in my lap. Never had I wanted sight more than at that moment.

"No," I whispered.

SUMMER BLAZED A blistering trail into August, school looming closer. I couldn't go. But I sat and sulked and never made the call.

I hadn't heard from Archer since April. Maybe things were getting better for him. Met someone, or at least thinking about dating, going out with friends.

Something heavy dropped onto the couch beside me. I jumped.

"Sorry," Shiloh said. "I figured you heard me coming down the stairs."

I heard everything. Why hadn't I heard her?

She sighed and flipped on the TV.

"How was work?" I asked.

"Like you care."

I leaned away.

She skimmed through channels for several minutes, then turned it off with another sigh. "God, you're stupid, Noah. I wish he'd asked me. What do you want? A fucking white horse?" She got up and walked away.

Luath and I listened to her go in silence.

I lay awake that night, clutching my old, private sketchbook, eyes closed, pretending I would open them to see Archer in the rain. I imagined I could see him beside me in bed, lying with my head on his chest, listening to his heart, kissing my way up his neck to his lips, though he didn't like it. He'd always been touchy about his neck. Yet he put up with me. He let me rest my fingertips against his lips while he spoke so I could see him talking. He took pictures of Luath for me to email her puppy raisers in California with detailed letters of her life and progress. He let me pick the carryout, or ate whatever I managed to cook, even the more suspect dishes. He gave me sight with his words, turned blank canvases into vivid paintings.

The next day, Saturday, once more alone with my dog, I called a cab.

With duffel bags and Luath in harness, I walked across the sidewalk to our little condo. She paused. I lifted my foot to the step. We stopped on the landing.

I reached to feel the door and knock. I had a key in my pocket but felt I had lost that privilege. I swallowed and waited, sweat breaking out on my neck and palms. Luath's body vibrated as footsteps approached from inside. Though she wagged her tail furiously, I knew that as long as she was working, she would not break her stance beside me without a release command to greet him.

The door opened.

Would he be willing to listen? Would he accept an apology? Would this even be him opening the door? Another man who'd been over for Friday night? What would I say? Why hadn't I thought this through? One word from Shiloh and I came running back after all those months? Stupid. Not thinking.

Archer threw his arms around me.

I dropped bags to hug him, shaking, ribs crushed by his arms and chest.

Luath stood against my left leg, tail and whole back end swinging.

"I'm so sorry," I said. "Yes. If the offer still stands."

He kissed me, hands on my face, fingers in my hair, body pressed against mine on the narrow landing. He stepped back, still holding my head, and kissed me again.

When I released Luath, she sprang at him, whimpering, and Archer knelt to hug her next.

FIRST SIGHT

Scene One

THE ROWS OF bodies look like so many Twinkies in their yellow robes, side by side, neat and orderly. They cover floor space in the abandoned house until investigators can scarcely find gaps to slip between each column.

From the decaying back deck, Dr. Chamaeleo looks in on the scene through a window thick in cobwebs and mildew. Only his eyes shift to follow men snapping pictures on digital cameras, inching about the devastation without disturbing a single robe.

Red and blue lights flash beyond windows from the suburban street out front. A dog barks. A muddled radio voice buzzes from the porch.

Robert Perth, chief of police, looks up from the open front door, all the way through the house to the window. The chief never knows that he looks right at Dr. Chamaeleo.

The next moment, Dr. Chamaeleo steps from rotting boards to hop an equally dilapidated fence into a weedy schoolyard. Breath steaming in an icy rain, he strides through frosty dandelions and flowerless Scotch broom, mind already racing ahead to finding Whiteout—the only person, living or dead, who could have arranged such a neat presentation.

Dr. Chamaeleo must stop at the drugstore for a card of congratulations. Then again, maybe Whiteout's last email address is still working.

Chapter One

"DR. CHAMAELEO?" ARCHER jabbed my shoulder with two fingers. "Really? How many superheroes or villains already exist who have chameleon or camouflage or shapeshifter abilities and names?"

"Meaning it's a classic," I said. "Who gets tired of shifters?"

"I don't know. You can do better, Noah. I thought you said you wanted to create a blind superhero. Where's that guy?"

I didn't answer for a minute, distracted by the plane's engine, voices of passengers concealed by the roar, and an infant crying a dozen rows ahead of us.

Archer shifted beside me, probably looking out the window. We had a whole row of three to ourselves, having followed advice from my father about booking a window and aisle seat toward the tail of the plane. The middle seat never sold, leaving us room to roam.

Archer insisted he wanted an aisle. He liked to be able to move. Really, I was beginning to wonder if he was claustrophobic. I had never known that about him. Maybe that was the point of these trips? Getting to know everything you had missed about one another before the vows.

Not as if I could enjoy the view, so he had taken the window while he could still see the vanishing Cascade Mountains or ocean or British Columbia. I wasn't even sure which direction the plane was taking. North or east?

I had badgered him to read the opening scene—first page, first draft—of my masterpiece in progress while we waited to board. We'd been interrupted by irksome matters like getting on the plane and settling in and taking off. After all the waiting, Archer had finally said something. Yet, now I had a funny feeling about the whereabouts of all that admiring praise I'd been expecting.

What if Archer did not appreciate how much work it had been, writing that first page?

"I did," I said about the hero question. "I just... I'm not sure—" I shrugged. "No one wants to read about a blind superhero."

"That's your motivation now? 'No one wants to read it'?" I could not hear Archer sigh over the noise of the plane, but I was sure he did. "I thought this was for fun. What difference does it make if nameless strangers want to read your comic book? One step at a time, Noah. Isn't the point of the outline writing what you care about? Next, you'll be telling me your hero isn't even gay."

"I just don't think blind will work." I felt into the now empty aisle seat to my right for my water bottle.

"That's mine," Archer said as I removed the cap.

"It is not. I tore the paper on mine so I could feel it." I drank. "You're such a dickhead sometimes."

He chuckled.

"What would I do besides enhanced non-sight senses? Hence, a Daredevil ripoff?" I asked, carefully twisting the cap back in place. "It's been done before. Anyway, don't you think a gay, blind superhero is a bit much?"

"Maybe for the 1970s. You just said it: so much has been done before. It's time for a blind gay superhero. Not to mention a few leading women who dress like normal people in safe, practical costumes. Not bras and shin guards to fight all the creatures of the underworld."

"Your views are too radical for today's fantasy audience—"

"First of all, that's not even true." Now he just sounded irritated. "There are a lot of smart people in the world who are fed up with panty heroines, and there are gay superheroes around already. Second, I told you to stop with the audience bit. If you're not doing this outline for yourself, who, exactly, are you writing for?"

I sat in silence, leaned close to him at the window so we could hear one another.

Of course I couldn't admit it, but that was a damn good question. When, and how, had I gotten it in my head that I wanted to develop my comic book idea with an artist and actually publish? I wasn't sure, but...there it was.

I had somehow regressed over ten years to junior high when I had read everyone from Chris Claremont to Jim Lee, Frank Miller, and Tim Truman, then drew and wrote my own, filling sketchbook after sketchbook. A long, long time ago. Yet, apparently, not as long as I'd led myself to believe.

So was I interested in seriously writing a comic book? Even if I could no longer be my own artist? Even if I had to collaborate with someone else, whose work I would never see? It sounded like a horrible idea. So I felt surprised to discover that I was unsure of the answer.

I said none of this to Archer. I had told him I wanted to do an outline just for fun and I'd welcome his feedback, and for now, that was the story I was sticking to. Trouble was, Archer hadn't given much feedback. Asking where the blind guy was and why I cared about a mythical audience? Not helping.

"Anything else?" I asked. "About the first page?"

"No."

"Except?" I prompted. I knew that tone.

"Except..." Maybe a shrug? "You know."

"No. That's why I asked for your feedback. I'm just starting outlines and scenes and characters. Now's the time."

"Well." Like a sentence. Like, *No*.

"Yes?"

"You know Whiteout is an office supply, right? No one is going to think of blizzards or anything if that's what you're going for."

"I thought of blizzards."

"And you used the word 'column' wrong. Column implies a vertical construct, not horizontal. And using Twinkies as a metaphor in your opening line sets a juvenile tone, don't you think? Unless your main character loves junk food and you're trying to develop him."

"Anything else?" I repeated, feeling stiff in my seat now. Yes, I wanted feedback, but this was minutiae. This stuff didn't matter. I wanted to know what he thought about the setup itself. The tension, drama, danger, and details. All those dead bodies.

"You said the weeds were 'frosty' or something in the same sentence you said it was raining. I guess that can happen, right at the moment it starts to rain and everything was already frosty, but it doesn't make sense. If you want to show how cold it is in the story, just note one: either freezing rain or frosty ground. Which one depends on the tone you're trying to set and the season."

What the hell did he know about tone and point of view? Archer didn't write. As far as I was aware, he had never shown the least interest in it either. I was the one into English and the classics. The one in school for it.

He might have grown up on some of the same comic books, but computers and games had been his thing.

I sat there, listening to the crying baby, not wanting to argue for the whole trip. Things had already been tense before we even reached security—when I thought I'd lost my passport. We both had to get them especially for this trip, neither having been outside the United States before.

"You're talking about trivialities," I said after a pause, trying not to sound too accusatory or snappish. "What about the overall concept? That's all that matters at this stage."

"Overall, okay, I guess. It's a little cliché, but if your hero is gay and blind and there's a fully dressed female lead, you can make up for it."

Nothing like a nice backhand to crown a heap of criticism.

"Thanks," I said stiffly.

Archer shifted beside me. "You said you wanted honest feedback, right? Not platitudes and pats on the back?"

"Sure. I'll think about the hero some more."

"You're really creative, Noah," Archer went on. "You wouldn't have any trouble with this if you did whatever you wanted. Don't worry about 'readers', or Daredevil, or that something's been done before. If you make it your own and do what inspires you, it's not going to matter. You'll do something great."

I leaned my head on his shoulder. "I'm sorry I called you a dickhead."

Archer chuckled. "You've called me worse."

"Then maybe I'm the dickhead."

"That seems more likely. Move. I'm going back to the aisle." Archer climbed over me, relocating our stuff from that seat, standing on my foot, and finally flopping back down. He let out a long breath that I could hear now. "Next stop, Amsterdam. Only ten short hours away."

"Can't wait." I leaned into him to kiss his jaw before resettling myself. "Happy honeymoon."

Chapter Two

FOR MOST OF the flight, I listened to audiobooks, though I could hardly pay attention. Instead, I thought of what Archer had said. The first step to writing the best comic book outline I could must be winning Archer over as a reader.

His lack of praise not only stung, but shocked me. It took me recalling showing him my artwork—sketchbooks, scraps, flip-book animations when we were in high school—to make me understand why.

Archer had loved my art. Besides being embarrassed and irritated when he realized how much I'd been sketching him, he had never said a bad thing about my work. But that was years ago. We were twenty-four now—him out of school, programming computers; me having gone back to school while still working my tele-jobs that long ago became my comfort zone. I hadn't drawn a picture in the past six of those years.

As the light had faded through the end of high school, while I lost my dreams of being a graphic artist, illustrator, or game animator, Archer had remained a source of constant encouragement—as well as the kinds of long, drawn-out sighs that made sight for reading expressions or body language unnecessary. A source of praise. But, unless it was about my pigheadedness or self-pity, he was not a source of criticism. I could always turn to my little sister, Shiloh, for that if needed.

Despite changing my interests from art to literature, now working on a BA in English to lead to an MA in world literature, I could not even impress my new husband with my own whimsical writing skills. My vague hope was to eventually be teaching the subject—although I'd never been a great planner and was taking my whole education one step at a time.

Archer's tepid reaction made me wonder anew if I wasn't deluding myself. When it came right down to it, I did not like English.

I'd been working at this college stuff for over a year and was still waiting for it to grow on me. What I cared about were the books. About classics—I had *Crome Yellow* , *A Soldier of the Great War*, *The Scarlet Letter*, and thirty more on my iPod just for this trip—and modern literature and journeys and feelings and characters. I didn't really give a damn about the hidden meaning behind every line, the social commentary that the author was allegedly making with each character, or anything else that involved dissecting a dazzling book like a stone-cold cadaver.

Not only was I failing to get into the spirit of analyzing every syllable of someone else's work, I'd also been getting flak about my own writing. Shouldn't that part of English study already be behind us?

I just didn't care whether or not there was always a comma before "too" at the end of a sentence, or if that was only old-fashioned nonsense. Did that comma, or lack thereof, ever change how anyone *felt* about a great story? If I had something to say, why couldn't I just say it?

Though frustrating, grammar and structure were rare reprimands compared to the suffering from chewing up and spitting out so many previously beautiful books. What used to be entertainment, a joy, had been militarized by a truckload of judgments aimed at every inch of a page until there was no way to get lost in a narrative.

Endless analyzing, as well as the rules I was apparently so lax on, had been crushing the English experience into a sham of classroom survival—having little to do with enjoying literature or eloquent expression in words.

By last summer, I'd decided to drop out.

Archer's encouragement and support—no surprise—got me back on campus in August. We had the wedding coming up by then. A blind guy with a minimum-wage job was one thing. I couldn't let Archer marry a dropout to boot.

My grades might be only so-so, but I could do this. At least for long enough to graduate and move on to purple pastures and sage skies. I hoped. What if the MA work was worse? No...then no one would do it.

After the abuse—and despite having no hidden story agenda to cryptically include between the lines myself—it had taken me a while to come to the conclusion that I could give personal writing a try. Although somewhat hamstrung by English, I'd finally taken that deep breath and jumped in. I had an idea for a comic book. I was going to write it.

Plowing through four times the number of books we were assigned to read by using increased playback speed on audiobooks allowed me to revisit favorites, assess what worked, and decide for myself. It wasn't as if dissecting them made them better books. No more than shaving a cat made it more adorable. But there was something else: not as if those greats, old or new, followed the rules either.

Which made the rules guidelines. Which meant that the rules really were bullshit. Which still didn't help me get better grades.

By this autumn, and our wedding day, I had been feeling much better about English. Maybe that was just because I was taking an extra long fall break for the honeymoon, or maybe it was because I felt liberated by all the notes I'd made about my comic story, even writing out the first scene. I was ready to embrace words in lieu of art once more. Comic books were my first love anyway—and perfect examples of not following rules.

So I had told Archer about my idea to try my own comic book treatment. In the whirlwind of the wedding, family, school, work, and leaving for this trip, I hadn't gotten very far. Still, I'd confidently pushed my little darling at him in the airport, all set for him to react to my clever first page as he used to react to my visual art.

Boom. As they would say in those jagged yellow boxes. *Smash! Crash!*

Damn. So it wasn't just that I didn't like picking apart other people's work. I sucked at it myself. What I was good at, what my life had laid out for me, was art. And that life was as dead as a raccoon on I-90.

Still, I couldn't be disheartened from one page and one critique.

By the time the nonstop flight reached the Netherlands, I had plans for my next scene and my hero to impress Archer.

The odd thing about us reaching the Netherlands was that, though we heard an announcement about being ready to land, and Archer moved back to the window to see, nothing else happened.

"What's going on?" I asked, aware of tense human silence in the cabin now. Not even children squalling.

Earbuds out, I leaned against him over the armrest between us, disconcerted by being unable to hear his breathing in the roaring plane.

He sat back from the window, more toward me. "Nothing but cloud out the windows. We must be circling the airport."

His words were hardly out when another announcement reached us, first in Dutch, then in English. Severe thunderstorms in Amsterdam had delayed both landings and takeoffs, so we had to wait in line at some distance before being allowed to land.

"Didn't we discuss weather?" I asked Archer, smiling.

Archer had every detail of this trip planned out. Yet he never mentioned lightning at Schiphol.

"Just a fluke," he said, again shifting away. "It'll clear up."

I heard many voices around us now, near and far, in Dutch, English, and one or two others. Many universal tones of surprise. *Thunderstorms over Amsterdam? In October?*

We waited. I went back to listening to Dickens on airplane mode since Archer was tensed up and not adding anything about the view. We waited more.

Ten minutes, half an hour.

No more hush on the plane. Infants crying, people arguing.

A solid hour we circled that airport. I was nearing the end of *Oliver Twist* when my stomach lurched and I knew we were finally descending.

Archer didn't warn me when the runway was approaching. I jumped and swore as Sikes ran from the crowd in my audiobook. I'd thought for a fraction of a second that we had hit something midair. Maybe a lightning bolt.

Archer did not bother apologizing either, but I left him alone. He didn't do well when his painstakingly laid plans got derailed by even a whisker.

As we taxied, I pulled the earbuds off and felt for the pouch to put everything back together in my carry-on.

Archer also put away and cleaned up, saying things like, "Finally," and, "The train into the city should be straightforward. Hopefully not affected by lightning."

Then we sat on the tarmac for an hour waiting for a gate.

Archer felt like a masseur's nightmare by the time we were at last allowed to stand up.

He hurried into the aisle and opened our overhead. It took me a while to stand, stretching and reaching with one hand for the low ceiling tucked back over the seats below a spout of cool air and round plaques, one of which feeling hot to the touch: reading light.

Archer pulled my hand away. "You'll be calling for an attendant in a minute."

"I have one." I smiled at his voice, though he sounded as rigid as he felt. "Deep breath, Archer. It's okay. What's the local time?"

"Seven at night. It's dark outside from the storm." He stopped as we all listened to a roll of thunder.

"Lightning?" I asked.

"Lots of flashes when we were out on the runway. Hardly anything now. Here." He pressed my collapsible white cane into my hand that he had pulled from the overhead, then my light Seattle rain jacket.

I wondered if it was going to be warm enough after all. Archer had assured me before setting out on this adventure that it would be mostly sunny and above 50°F in Amsterdam for our stay.

I rested the cane on the seat and pulled on my jacket, then my backpack with his help. Archer readied himself in the aisle while I listened to the tight, close crowd talking or waiting in frazzled silence like stretched fishing line, ready to snap.

"Moving ahead," Archer warned me, hand on my elbow.

"You better open this so I don't clobber anyone."

He opened the cane for me and pressed it back to my fingers as I stepped into the crammed aisle with him, moving in front of him in line. I found my way with the feel and sound, touching sides of seats and aisle carpet with the cane. Archer kept his hand on my waist like a dancer, pushing me slightly ahead as there was space.

He warned me about the turn to the hatch, thanked our flight attendant—I assume that was who he spoke to—and we stepped out into balmy, wet air like a rainy day in Florida. Not, so we'd heard, like the Netherlands in autumn.

Archer stepped up beside me as we entered the loading gate corridor and we could walk side by side. I switched my cane to my left hand, the strap around my wrist, and held Archer's left elbow with my right hand.

His breathing was rapid, the mass of footsteps sounding hollow and endless around us. Another roll of thunder cut in. The floor below my shoes and swollen feet felt like a board of plastic over open air, giving under pressure just enough to be disturbing at each step. Everything smelled of dampness and rubber and other human beings. Noise of rain hammered just overhead.

I wished desperately for Luath as I walked with the stiff and silent Archer.

I had received my first guide dog just a few years ago but had hardly been parted from her since then. This, Archer and I had both known, would be too much. Luath was staying with my mom and sister, who was working and living at home in Olympia. Luath loved them. Shiloh would take her for walks and entertain her. But I knew Luath would miss her work as much as I missed her.

"Right," Archer said.

We turned right and walked up a long ramp, made a U-turn to the left, then up another, then a sharp right and out into a whole new feel and sound and space.

The rain noise vanished. The floor was solid linoleum. Now other humans were at a respectful distance. Hum and murmur and electric buzz. Thousands of walking feet. Relatively fresh air. Hint of coffee and newsprint and some kind of food in the background. Something hot and greasy. Those famous Holland fries? More likely a terminal McDonald's.

Archer pulled me to one side. "Okay?"

I nodded. "I'm fine. Didn't know it would be so warm."

"Okay," he said again, letting out a breath. Off plan, but recoverable.

I, personally, was not worried about our plans. We'd get there when we got there. But I would have given fifty bucks for a bathroom right then.

"We have to get the checked bag, then find the trains. All the signs I can see from here are in English, so should be no problem. Come on." As we set out through the terminal, he added, "And a restroom on the way to baggage claim."

"You read my mind. What about customs?"

"I'm not sure if that's before or after we get the bag."

Archer had the travel bug since I'd known him. But that didn't mean he did it. We had both flown—family visits, one or two domestic vacations. That was about it.

As we waited in line at customs—another long wait and, thankfully, post-bathrooms—I began to wonder for the first time if our inexperience might actually be a problem.

What if we said something stupid to a customs agent and they...did whatever they do? Pulled us out of line? Locked us up?

What if they didn't speak English? What if we were separated? What if they didn't like Americans? Didn't like gays? Didn't like our bags or our haircuts or the brands of our shoes or blind people?

As it turned out, the friendly woman's voice asked how long we intended to stay, taking both our passports, stamped or punched something on paper by the sound, then told us to enjoy our visit to Amsterdam. She sounded like she could be from LA.

Archer handed me back my passport, which I zipped into my inside coat pocket. It was getting to be stifling. I needed to take the thing off.

"See?" I said to him, smiling as we went on.

"It's always weird when you say that," Archer said.

"Smooth sailing from here in."

"Here *on*, not here *in*," he corrected me.

"Any chance of something to eat before baggage claim?" I asked.

"I just want to get out of here. There should be food around the trains."

So we went straight to collect our one checked bag, which was split with both our clothes while we each carried a personal bag. As I had told Archer, when you don't take a dog or a sister with you, it's easy to pack light.

Down in another crowd, bags already rolling on a grinding conveyor belt, then thump and bang of suitcases being fountained out.

"Want to sit down for a minute? I'll grab it."

"I didn't guess you'd send me to fetch it," I said. "But I've had enough sitting. Somewhere I can stand and not be trampled?"

Archer led me to a supportive pillar in the open, rumbling vastness of space around me.

"Here." He guided me until I could touch it with my shoulder. "You're facing the belt from our flight. Just wait a minute and I'll be right back."

"Aye, aye." Cane in my hand, I stood with the solid column for several minutes, thinking about bodies and Twinkies.

Fifteen minutes, maybe more. Beginning to wonder. Then Archer returned.

"Haven't seen it. Sorry, Noah. There must be more still below."

But the thumping and banging of more bags being sent up had stopped ten minutes ago.

"It's okay." I felt like my stomach was going to fall through my backbone. A Twinkie had never sounded so good. Though I'd prefer a Caesar salad with grilled chicken and extra croutons, and a peanut butter milkshake. "It'll turn up. It was a nonstop flight. It's not like they lost it."

Another wait. The noise faded. The grating machine stopped.

"Archer?"

His breathing was shallow and rapid beside me. "No bag."

"Huh." I just stood there. "Easier to get around on the train."

"That's not funny, Noah."

"Could we get something to eat before we start asking people from the airline about it?"

"We can't ask anyone. The lost baggage check and other stations down here are closed for the evening."

"All the more reason to go ahead and get something to eat."

Archer sighed.

Chapter Three

THROUGHOUT ARCHER'S EFFORTS to report the missing bag, we still had nothing to eat. I had moved on from the Caesar salad and decided just a corn chip was sounding pretty damn delicious.

Plenty of food through the terminal, on the way to train tickets—smells of cooked meats, pastries, even seafood. Nearly all closed, Archer told me.

After customs, waiting for the bag, trying to ask around and get help, finding that no one else knew anything about the bag, then running to get train tickets, it was well past 9:00 p.m. local time. We had been up for twenty-four hours.

The storm had subsided to a steady downpour, and Archer was informed, again in perfect English, now by a male voice, that the trains were running fine. There was one for Amsterdam Central Railway in five minutes—just downstairs, platform four. No time to find anyone serving those fries or anything else.

Archer all but ran to the noise of humming engines and dank, sharp, metallic odors.

"Escalator. You go first, here." He guided my hand to the moving rubber rail. "Step."

I felt and stepped, again with Archer's hand on my waist. I much preferred elevators, but he must have been in too much of a hurry to wait for one.

He warned me at the bottom and I felt with the cane, then took his arm before he hurried down a great tunnel of nothing. Oppressive, ringing with engines and footfalls and voices. No moving air. Sounds and smells trapped around us by solid walls, presumably of concrete.

Few people at first, then others swarmed into us. Leather, perfume, aftershave, sweat, and cigarette smoke. Someone brushed against me, going the other way. Yet I could feel a wave of them just out of reach. A small crowd which must have been disembarking our train.

Archer hurried forward, almost jogging, and I wanted to tell him to stop, my heart pounding with the sheer unfamiliarity of the place. I hadn't minded the airport. I had been in airports. This, though... Now I was in a foreign country.

Archer swore under his breath, stopping short. My cane tapped into an expanse of nothing, dropping without a step, just open air. Side to side: nothing. Up: nothing. A sweeping, empty blank. Like an elevator shaft without the elevator.

Mouth dry and heart hammering even faster, I clutched Archer's arm.

"It's the gap between the train and the platform," Archer said. "Up more."

I raised the stick farther. *Click.* Touching steel. The underside of the step to the train car.

"It's six or eight inches out and twice as high as a normal stair step. Once you're on it, there are three more steps to the top."

"We climb up...into the train?" I asked.

"It's a double-decker train."

"What?"

When I hesitated, Archer pulled me forward.

"That's what it is," he said. "Like the red busses in England."

"No..."

"It is, Noah. It's crazy. I've never seen anything like it."

"How do you get a suitcase or a wheelchair on?"

"There are other doors along the train where you step down instead of up. Go on." Tone sharp then. "It's already supposed to be going."

I stepped out into the void, up, up, finally, after hitting it with my toe, I felt the solid step. Archer pushed my hand to a cold rail. I stepped and stumbled in, nearly knocked down by the height of the steps tripping me, clutching the rail instead of Archer, while he followed.

The door slid shut behind us—automatically, I assumed.

Archer panted, holding onto my wrist as we stood on a metal surface in a tight space. I could feel a wall at my side. Openness ahead and to the right, Archer to the left.

"We're, uh, in, uh...thing." It wasn't like Archer to fall down on descriptions, but I cut him some slack, my own hands shaking. "We can go up a few stairs to the upper... deck, or down a few to a car with seats in little compartments with plexiglass or something around them."

"Why does it stink?" I smelled mildew and rust and a million phantoms of human, food, and smoke—even dog.

"Probably because it's about eighty years old."

Wham. The floor lurched below us and I fell into Archer, knocking him sideways. He must have steadied himself on something because he didn't go far. The train shuddered as it rolled out.

"A split-level," I said, trying to catch my own breath.

"What? Oh, yeah, that's exactly what it's like. Like being just inside the front door of a split-level house."

"Up?" I proposed. "The plexiglass cages sound creepy."

Archer led me up several more stairs to odorific fabric seats in a drafty car that swayed in an unsettling way toward Amsterdam—I hoped.

"We're underground, below the airport," Archer said. "I can't see a thing through the windows." He was speaking under his breath, hardly loud enough for me to hear. "It's got to be the right train. That guy said platform four."

We never were able to confirm the train, just riding along on faith. And Archer never was able to see much of our arrival to his beloved—in fantasy only—city of canals and history. Between the pouring rain and being dark out, he said he could hardly see a thing even pulling into Amsterdam Central.

"How can they have lost our bag?" he said four or five times, while all I could think about was starvation and passing out from a low blood sugar attack. Was that the smell of something fried? "No change, one airline, one plane. How the hell'd they lose our bag?"

"We might get it back. Hear from them tomorrow—"

"I doubt it. And what are we going to do if we don't?"

"Go around naked? I think that's legal here..."

Archer sighed.

"I'm sorry, Archer. I'm really, really tired and hungry and don't know what to tell you." And scared. I couldn't say it to him, but that train platform had been shit scary. Archer usually got it. He gave a lot of warning. He knew there were challenges. But today hadn't been a "usually" kind of day.

It wasn't over. Out of the crowded station. All places of nourishment closed. Then another light rail conveyance or streetcar of some kind—more steps up—after being yanked by Archer through the rain. The temperature had dropped now, and I was glad of the jacket. Wished I had more.

I wanted to ask if there was anything to eat outside of the station, but I could tell Archer was on too much of a fixed mission to stop for trifling life necessities like food, even if there was a restaurant open.

By asking two passengers on the next bus-like conveyance for help, Archer discovered we wanted off on a stop called Weteringcircuit, then still had a good walk ahead of us to reach our accommodation. From there, Archer could see on his phone we had something like six blocks to go on Stradhouderskade—which neither of us tried to say, though he spelled for me—past the Rijksmuseum, then left at the panhandle of the park, Vondelpark, and another block or so to the final destination.

"Is there anything to eat over there?" I asked hopefully of our aids on the streetcar or whatever we were on, my head bowed beside Archer.

"Everything. It's a huge shopping area. A good place to stay," a woman said.

"The Hard Rock Cafe is across the street from the park," a man said. Clearly, he thought we Americans would like that.

Archer thanked them.

Yes, just what we needed. Halfway around the world to eat at a Hard Rock Cafe. Well, I would take it. Or even the McDonald's that I thought I'd smelled.

"At least everyone speaks English," I said to Archer after we stepped off our ride and he stood with me for a moment to get his bearings, presumably looking at the digital map. "And it would have sucked getting the suitcase onto and off of these trains and trams anyway."

"Thank you, Pollyanna." Archer's voice was flat. "I'll keep that in mind while I'm walking around nude in the rain and cold in the days to come. All right." He turned against me, orienting himself. "This way."

Chapter Four

I DID NOT realize until we stepped out that the rain was still falling. We must have been under a shelter at the stop. Holding onto Archer's arm, I used my cane hand to fumble my hood up.

Sounds of urban traffic everywhere, plus feet and voices.

I was used to the city. Archer and I lived in the University District in Seattle. I was no stranger to damp, cold weather either. And hearing foreign languages around me, of which I knew not a single word—Archer had made an effort to memorize a few polite phrases in Dutch before coming—was not so distressing as long as I had him there. It was my own reeling fatigue and the feeling that I had somehow been tricked about the time that was unsettling. This rumbling, bustling, chatting, humming city did not sound like 10:00 p.m.

"Archer?" I said, fighting my hood up as we moved off. "Are you sure it's night?"

"*Believe me.* Dark as—" He stopped after only three steps. "Hang on. Curb down and we have to cross the street. We're on some kind of median."

"They drop off people in the middle of the road?"

"Looks like it. Okay, come on." He started but stopped again after only a few steps as a great jingling of bells blared and something whooshed past. "*What the—?*"

He pushed me a step back, then forward at a run, yanking me through rain and noise—"Curb!"—cane hitting, stepping up.

"Sorry, Noah. Are you okay?"

"I'm fine."

"It was a bike. Guy didn't even have a light on it." Archer paused, breathing quickly by my face. "They're all over. More on the other side of the traffic circle, or whatever it is we were dropped on. And at the intersection. It looks like we're in a busy hub. I knew Amsterdam was famous for the bikes, but what are they doing out in the middle of the night in the rain without lights? You'd think being known for something and being good at it would go hand in hand."

We started off again as he spoke. Archer always thought people had, or would use, much more common sense than they do—perpetually shocked by the stupid things other people do without it crossing their minds that anything is amiss. I was not surprised by lightless bikes. I used to ride a bike myself, and I never imagined there was any chance I would be hit by a car or need to warn people out of my own way. Archer thought too much.

"Okay." Shaking himself, he led me on what must have been a city sidewalk, uneven and climbing a slight hill. "We're walking past a little park on the right. The street on the left. There's a canal just ahead and we're coming up on the bridge over. Considering we're in a huge metropolitan city, it's really dark. There are streetlights and headlights and windows, but there's hardly anything in this park. And it's not like there are neon signs or skyscrapers with every window lit. Amazing, how it really does still feel ancient. I've never seen anything like it." Finally getting excited now, even in the rain and night, able to realize he had landed for his dream trip.

"Imagine it in the morning." My teeth chattered. "It'll get better and better."

"Now, we're going right, but if we went on, diagonally on the left is the Heineken headquarters. Or just a beer tourist trap. I'm not sure that is the headquarters... It's all lit up anyway. Turn. We're on a sidewalk along that street now."

"The one with the S name?"

"Yes. Canal on our right, storefronts and restaurants and bars are across the street to the left. That's the busy sidewalk over there. We need to cross at some point. I can't believe how dark it is on this side—" He jumped as another bell blared behind us, yanking my arm so hard I almost fell, staggering with him into a curb.

"Archer! Are we walking in the street?" My heart was pounding again as I felt the bicycle zip past my elbow.

"What the hell—?" He pushed me back, sideways, tripping on what I thought was a curb, but seemed to be only a jutting brick. "We're not in the road. The crazy biker was on the sidewalk."

Brring brrring ring.

More bikes, two or three or four, darting past through the rain.

"Fuck," Archer panted. Not like him.

I was more prone to dramatic language. Archer was raised without being permitted to see PG-13 movies until he was actually thirteen years old. And he'd been the kind of kid who didn't see movies that he wasn't supposed to either.

"Should we cross the street? Or can we just move over?" I was feeling around that erroneous brick to find a soft patch of ground beyond. I jerked my foot away. "Is that dirt?"

"There's a little tree. They're along here, above the canal." He stuck out his arm as if pointing.

"Big help." My hands shook even worse as I held him and the cane, not sure if it was more from cold or fatigue or starvation or building terror.

"I can hardly see it in the rain," Archer said. "I told you it's super dark. There's a bike lane over here."

"All the more reason for the assholes not to come up on the sidewalk."

"No, I mean, it's on the sidewalk. Half is for the bikes, I guess."

"What?"

"That's what it looks like. But…what's on the other side is the canal. There's no wall, no fence, there's not so much as a rope like the ones at art museums that your mom was always taking you to. So…if you have to dodge a bike, you'd go right in."

"How far down?"

"I can't tell. Maybe…five or six feet to the water from where we are now. And they're mostly not deep, so technically, I guess you'd live if you fell in. I can't imagine how you'd get out, though, even if you could stand up."

"We need to cross the street."

More bikes and bells flitted past.

"So many people over there," Archer said. "We'd have a hard time maneuvering."

"As opposed to what we're doing now?"

We had to go on with the canal side just to find a crosswalk with a light. The nighttime traffic was such, and the bikes were so random, that Archer would not hear of jaywalking. Even when he told me we had a green light, he moved with caution.

The canal sidewalk had been so rough and uneven, jagged with bricks or cobbles or whatever was jutting up from pressure of tree roots or time, I had tripped and stumbled all along that side anyway. Now, the sidewalk almost felt normal under my thin-soled shoes that allowed me to feel my place in the world—but the walk itself was just as stressful.

Archer kept pulling up, pushing me aside, stopping or slowing, then suddenly speeding up. For a long time, though, he sounded breathless and his arm was rigid under my hand. Archer tried to commentate for me.

"There's a stop for canal tour boats—watch it! And we're coming up to the Rijksmuseum. Wow, Noah, it's amazing—hold on. It's like the most incredible gothic, medieval cathedral, or tower, anything you could ever imagine. It's like a castle—curb."

Pretty soon, he wasn't saying anything, just pulling me on while I felt with the cane at the same time. I thought of missing home and bed, Caesar salads and pizza, and mostly my dog. But could she have even handled this?

Finally, panting, also shaking, Archer pulled up short and did not start off again. He turned. I waited.

"I don't see the street sign. There's the Hard Rock...but... This is Hobbemastraat..." He drew the word out with precision. "And we're looking for Vossiuss—" He gave up finishing that one. "Anyway, where—?"

"Just ask someone, Archer. I'll ask someone." I didn't care. I'd talk to anyone. Due to my mother's starting me as her main salesperson at markets and craft shows where she sold her art the whole time I was growing up, I had no problem with introduction-discomfort like Archer did. I wasn't sure if shy was the right word for him. Maybe just...aloof.

"Let's check down here—"

"Archer, really. We have to ask someone—"

"There. I think this is it."

Another street to cross. My cane caught a rail for a streetcar embedded in the road itself and was nearly whipped out of my hand. More staggering and Archer getting us to another curb.

"Yes. Here we go. A block down and we're there."

This sidewalk was so narrow, Archer kept reprimanding me for trying to stay beside him and to hang back instead. If I didn't, I would hit jutting steps up to doors of homes and inns.

He let out his breath.

"Here?" I asked.

"We're here. And only...five hours later than planned."

"Is there anything to eat on this street?"

"Not that we passed. But lots just off that main drag we turned from. We'll ask inside about what's open. I don't even know if I can eat, though."

I knew what he meant. I was starting to feel beyond hunger and more than beyond relieved. The thought of setting back out into the carnage was alarming at best.

"All right, steps," he said.

I felt with the cane up bricks. Six steps to a landing.

My hand still on his soaked jacket sleeve, Archer pulled open a door and we walked into a gust of warm air without rain or bike bells or traffic or feet. Instead, a wave of blasting music and laughing voices bore witness to the party inside.

Chapter Five

"WE'RE HERE TO check in." Archer's voice was ahead of me before I could gape and point out that he had not told me this was a party hostel.

He had done so much research before getting on that plane that it was hard to believe he never saw that in any online reviews. Even harder to believe he would have booked it if he'd known.

"Archer Lucassen and Noah Pearce," Archer went on.

We had debated the names before the wedding. No power struggle bullshit. Just that neither one of us wanted to change to the other's name. Maybe if we'd been planning to raise kids—and I did think Archer would be a great dad—but no chance of that, so there never seemed to be much reason that one of us had to compromise in the name department when we both wanted our own.

"Fill this out, please. Signatures here. And I'll get your keys." Again, I was taken aback by the perfect English. I could scarcely detect an accent on this woman, who must've been behind a counter.

I stood by Archer, wishing someone would kill the music so I could hear actions around me.

"Is this your first time to Amsterdam?" She sounded close, just past Archer, and chipper for 10:30 p.m.

"Yes," I called back over the noise. "Just here from the airport and we haven't eaten in about fifteen hours. Anything really fast and simple right around here that's still open?"

"What do you like?"

"Are there options with all three of those priorities?" I asked.

She laughed. "Go to Wagamama. Did you see the Hard Rock Cafe coming in?"

I was never sure if they were asking me or Archer when they said something like that. It wasn't an expression like *See what I'm saying?* But it could mean, in context, *Are you aware of/Did you notice?* It didn't always mean *Did you "see" it?*

Still, unless I was in what Archer called a "snark" mood, I tended to avoid answering such questions and let them go to him.

No telling if this woman had even clued in to me yet. I went in for the dark glasses sometimes, out on the street with Luath, maybe in class, but not for this travel day. They made me feel more comfortable because people couldn't tell I wasn't meeting their eyes when they talked to me. And just to look cool myself. Though I wasn't terribly self-conscious about the appearance of my eyes to others. Aggressive retinitis pigmentosa had drawn a film over them, darkening and obscuring until there was nothing left for me to see. My eyes might look different from the outside as well, but hardly as if I sent children screaming and running from me on the streets.

This time, Archer did not answer for me with the "did you see" question. He was filling in our check-in paperwork. After a beat, I answered.

"He saw it." Still having to speak loudly. "What's Wagamama?"

"It's a Japanese noodle place. They'll get you a meal fast and you're in luck because they're open really late on Fridays. I can show you on the map." Paper sounds behind the booming rock music and jolly crowd around a corner.

"Thanks. That sounds perfect." Not easy to eat. Pizza; easy. Chicken fingers; easy. Something about ramen noodles and spaghetti and meatballs just has not agreed with me as much since I haven't been able to see the bowl. Still, food would be warm and comforting if it was really so close to get to.

"You need to sign this, Noah." Archer's hands on mine, clipboard, paper, pen into my fingers while the light cane dangled from my wrist. "From here." Placing the tip of the pen for me.

Our hostess waited for him. She had obviously caught on by now and did not seem to be trying to show me the Japanese place on a map.

Archer passed her back the objects he had pushed at me. They talked about maps, room keys, towels and linens, and getting on WiFi. Then Archer explained about our missing bag and that he'd given people at the airport his number but also the hostel's, not sure if his phone would work for them.

She was all sympathy and assurances that they would take messages and let us know. Not as bubbly and laughy anymore. A little too much sympathy.

I hate pity. From strangers, that is. As Archer has eagerly pointed out, I can wallow all I want and enjoy it. My mother can look after me and cook for me. My sister can take care of my dog. Not strangers. Archer was never one for pity—giving it, I mean. In our teens, when he found me ready to curl up into a ball and die over beginning to lose my sight, he had told me to grow some.

We took the stairs—no elevator in the place—up to the third-floor room. Nothing but a muddle, following Archer without any sense of the building besides lots of stairs.

We dumped our bags in the private hostel room and washed our hands in the hall bathroom. Now just passports and wallets still on us with room keys and phones.

Archer hesitated in the hall.

"Noah, are you sure...?"

I knew he didn't want to go back out. "We've got to eat something, Archer. Come on."

"I could..." But he stopped again and led me back down all those steps.

Another alarming trip, though short, not so much noise now. No bike bells, hardly anyone rushing past as it neared 11:00 p.m. and the rain grew thicker all the time.

We ate delicious bowls of gingery rice noodles in flaming broth with chicken and cucumbers and I don't know what was on them. I struggled with the invisible noodles falling off my chopsticks and burning broth scalding my tongue.

Finally, I asked Archer if he would be embarrassed if I put my face down to the bowl.

"Noah, I wouldn't be embarrassed if you sat in it. I'm so, so tired." He sounded like a zombie, just enough life left to groan out the words. "There's hardly anyone even in here. They're closing up."

I leaned down, nose into the bowl, and lifted the long noodles from there. Much easier. And safer.

Another trip to the hostel, pelting down rain.

More stairs. And more.

Returned to the dry room, we faced the dilemma of what we did and did not have. I had a toothbrush. Archer did not. I had underwear. Archer did not.

"Didn't you pack anything useful in your carry-on?" I asked as Archer dug through his messenger bag beside me.

"Of course I did. Everything I would need on an airplane."

I sat on one of the little beds while he stood, opening zippers and pulling things out. A twin room. Queen beds don't seem to be a common option in the hostel world. Or en suite. Or much in the way of catering to honeymooning couples. At least this was only two twins and not two bunk beds, which was the next option.

"You can borrow my toothbrush," I told him as he remained silent and digging in tired frustration.

"I don't want your toothbrush. I'll just use some of your toothpaste and rinse my mouth. We'll have to buy stuff tomorrow. It's going to be half our budget for the whole time here."

Probably not an exaggeration.

"I'm sorry," I said.

Archer grabbed my hand to lead me out to the bathrooms, down the hall—which is a shitty thing to do and he knew it. It's not pleasant to be dragged around by the hand when you cannot see where you're going. I hold my guide. They don't hold me. If they do, a shoulder or upper arm is much more appreciated than having my hands controlled. Obviously, Archer knew this. He must have been too tired to care just then. And, it turned out...so was I.

Speaking of shitty things related to blindness: public restrooms. This wasn't so bad, being semiprivate and well kept. Not like it was in the mall or a service station. Still, got to be one of the least pleasant places in the world to have to feel your way around.

Archer sounded drugged as he mumbled the layout to me. A couple of urinals and couple of toilet stalls on one side; sinks, mirrors, counter space for toiletry bags and shaving gear by the door; and three shower stalls on the other side beyond a saloon-style swing door.

I didn't even have the ambition to ask about colors as I managed to wash my face with hand soap and brush my teeth. Colors were important to me. Archer usually made a point of mentioning paint or decor or fabric colors.

Back in our little room, I had nothing to sleep in. I only felt my way to the bed opposite the one with our bags on it, sat on the edge, pulled off everything but briefs, and crawled into bed.

It felt like a pad of cotton on plywood. But it also felt like lying down—like sleep.

Archer crept in against me a moment later, not technically fitting in the shared space, but close enough. He'd intended to push the two beds together. One more thing we couldn't be bothered about at midnight.

He kissed me but had to turn his back to me, my back being right against the wall in order to give us enough space for him not to fall off. I put my arm around his chest, my own voice startling me, I was already so far gone.

"Supposed to be the first night...honeymoon...bed..." All I could manage.

"Like...fasting," Archer murmured. "Makes it...better later."

We had already been living together, some of that on-again, off-again, for a few years before the wedding of a few days ago.

"Thank you, Archer...being here."

"Love you," Archer answered, and if he said anything else, I didn't hear it.

Chapter Six

I WOKE SEVERAL times in the night. Vague, uneasy wakings, not fully conscious, yet aware of a great deal of noise. Archer slept close against me, my arm still around him in the little bed. Those muffled voices belonged to others. All that shifting and thumping came from beyond a dampening barrier.

Amsterdam. We were in Amsterdam. I was working on my comic book idea. There was a hellish long flight—coming on Archer's dream trip. Dreaming. Maybe that was all.

Just dreaming. Otherwise, who could be making all that noise? For that matter, who would go to Amsterdam for a honeymoon instead of to a white sand beach? Who would go to a youth hostel instead of a charming bed-and-breakfast with a water view?

I smiled against Archer's shoulder. A view? Such a comedian. That's what I should be doing—polishing my act rather than paying for lectures on metaphor and simile, theme and symbolism.

Next time I woke, I really was awake. Something loud, a great *bang*, had shocked me into almost starting up from bed. I shivered, held onto Archer, and listened. It was times like those when I longed to reach out and turn on a lamp, just for a quick look around.

Voices beyond walls and doors. Another bang, farther away, not so startling. Doors being slammed shut. People in and out of rooms down the hall.

Amsterdam. Remember. Again. Disconcerting nevertheless.

I curled closer into Archer, my face against his neck—a trick to fool my brain into believing my eyes were choosing to be shut and hiding in the dark. If I really wanted to look around, check out those noises, I could. But I would rather be in bed, holding onto my new husband, who obviously wasn't concerned—or even awake?

White sand beach versus Amsterdam. So much better than any beach because this was what Archer wanted. I wouldn't say no to a beach, but travel was no longer much of a draw for me. Archer always wanted to travel, had a priority list since I'd met him—Amsterdam, Paris, London, Galapagos Islands, Bhutan, Scotland, plus all over our own country—especially New York City and San Francisco. Why exactly those places, I was not sure. Only that Archer wanted to see everywhere and those destinations somehow reached the top.

Voices fading. Then nothing but distant murmurs. Go back to sleep.

Instead of sleep, thinking of travel. Breathing against Archer's skin, then wiggling down enough to press my ear to his upper back so I could listen to him. His lungs and heartbeat sounded like they always had in Seattle. My only familiar sound besides his voice since we had arrived.

Archer's love of travel was only one of many reasons I'd refused when he first proposed. I couldn't let a man who considered travel one of his biggest goals to be saddled with a blind guy for the rest of his life. I'd known that plenty of blind people were avid travelers, even mountaineers and marathon runners and anything else you could imagine. I just wasn't one of them. Not yet. Likely never. I'd still rather read about someone else doing that stuff, preferably with rich visual descriptions worked into the text.

With a final "Yes" leading us toward a final "I do," I knew Archer and I had to travel somewhere wonderful for the honeymoon. Archer was too practical to have yet visited any of his top places—frugal, thoughtful, careful.

I was the one who had asked our parents—Archer's mom and my divorced set—to buy us the roundtrip tickets as their wedding gift, much to the befuddlement of all three. *You want to go where?*

But, even after the tickets, the cost of staying in the city was shocking. As much for a week as we spent in a month of rent, and that was for the cheap stuff.

Archer had only proposed the hostel idea in jest: "If we stayed in a hostel, we could afford to eat while we're in the city."

"Why can't we?" I'd asked.

He had laughed. "Come on, Noah. For a honeymoon? A hostel?"

"Would you rather stay in a hostel in Amsterdam for your honeymoon, or in a sweet bed-and-breakfast on the Washington coast?"

So Holland won.

By this latest time of waking up, I was beginning to suspect Archer had indeed known it was a party hostel and went for it anyway based on overall reviews, location, and price.

I didn't mind. And I didn't mind hosteling in general. And I didn't mind the delays and the storm. And the bag...not as if there had been family relics in it.

What I did mind was remembering how Archer had hesitated about going back out, wanted to ask me something, or tell me to...stay behind? He must have been about to say that. Because what I minded most of all was how hard it had been to get around in this city so far. Could more of this place be even worse? Maybe impossible?

Yes, the dream destination. Might as well prioritize. But...what if this dream was turning into a nightmare? What if Amsterdam wasn't going to prove to Archer that he really could have it all—and me that I could be all he wanted in a partner—but instead do the opposite? Prove that Archer was tied down? Prove that I could never travel to these places?

Only one evening so far. We'd been here a matter of hours. Surely the city wouldn't go on trying to kill us by daylight and with all our wits about us.

Don't panic over this. Just starting. In more ways than one.

Still, it was a while before I could once more drift off.

The next disturbance to wake me was Archer moving away. It should not have, but feeling him vanish made me panic.

"Wait, Archer." Reaching for him, I was still mostly asleep.

He sat on the edge of the little bed, inches from me. I felt his warm side, skin over his ribs, down to his waist. I tried to drag him back.

"Just going to shower," he mumbled.

"What time is it?"

"Their time, it's six in the morning." He went on, as if to himself. "We should shop for a couple things, toothbrush and underwear and razors and stuff today."

"No rush for that. Stay in bed a few more hours and be jet-lagged." When I could not get him back to me, I pulled myself against him, kissing his spine, wrapping my arms around him.

It wasn't all that simple for me. I couldn't just shop for a safety razor and count my blessings. I used an electric one and a particular system so I'd been able to learn to shave without assistance. Archer knew this well, but he probably thought I'd let him help me in a pinch. I'd rather just not shave for a while, although…the whole trip? Wouldn't be looking much like my passport photo by the time we started for home.

I didn't mention the shaving.

"Who knows how easy it will be to find stuff around here, though." Archer yawned and covered my hand with his. "I'm predicting a very long day."

"We knew the first day was a wash," I said, suppressing my own yawn. "Why are you getting up so early? We need a little time to recover and drink a lot of water."

"Speaking of which, I have a headache. I was falling down on that yesterday. And I can't get back to sleep. You stay in bed if you like."

"I need to come shower with you. I won't be able to figure it out on my own."

Archer stretched, moving his hand off mine and extending his arms until I heard his shoulders pop, feeling the strain through his back.

"Come on then. No one will be in there now. Not after everyone else in this place was up until about two hours ago." He had noticed as well.

I kissed him again, skin warm and familiar. "Party hostels are good places to meet other young travelers."

"Ones who can relate to us, I'm sure. I bet there are a bunch of couples here on their honeymoons." He sighed, which made me feel better—such a classic mode of communication for him.

We pulled on jeans from the previous travel day, Archer passed me towels to carry, and we made our way to the shower room.

Archer, keeping his voice down and still not in much of an explanation mood, told me that the three shower stalls had doors like typical toilet cubicles in public bathrooms. Except that these doors were much smaller. They were plastic, while the floor and walls of the stalls were tile. We would have to use hand soap from the sinks since we didn't have anything else besides my mini toothpaste.

We had bathroom and shower flip-flops to wear in these communal places—in our checked bag. I knew walking into the bathroom and tile shower stall barefoot would be setting Archer's teeth on edge, but he said nothing.

I assumed we could share one of those stalls and a bottle of soap.

Apparently not. If I'd thought marriage would make Archer more comfortable with public displays of affection, I was also mistaken.

Even at 6:00 a.m., still reeling and with a headache, the thought that some frat party insert-nationality-here guys could walk into this room and see we were in a shower together left him tetchy. Which shouldn't have been a big deal. As it turned out, however, Archer's unwillingness to share a shower soon unfolded into the greatest stress of the trip so far.

Chapter Seven

I FELT MY way into the narrow space, pulled the flapping door after me, then felt around three tiled walls.

Archer, with the soap bottle in the stall next to mine, said, "On the opposite wall to the door is a...thing." There was a pause. Then the sound of running water and Archer cursing and gasping. "Push on the metal thing, but get up against the wall before you do because it sprays cold water when it starts."

"Does it warm up?" My teeth were already chattering.

"Uh..."

I felt again across the back wall. And again, back and forth, farther down, then up. Cold tile, rough grout, and who knew what all nameless bacteria living on the stuff I was compelled to fondle like a cashmere sweater.

"Archer, this is stupid. Where is it?"

"Right in the middle of the wall. Yes, it warms up." The sound of the spray next door ceased. "And shuts itself off," Archer added.

Water started again.

I faced the back wall, extended both hands, and lined myself up evenly. I reached straight out. Tile. Down, down, nothing. Up, up, up—side of my hand brushing something even more cold and smooth. A stainless steel knob or button. I stood back at the inside corner of the stall to press on it. Nothing happened. I pressed again.

Archer's water shut off next door, then restarted.

I pressed several times fast and the water burst on over my head. My location was insufficient for my own protection and I was sprayed by icy drops. Clenching my teeth, I tried to get even farther away. In a moment, the thing reached room temperature. And switched itself off.

I turned it back on. Now warming up. I stepped under, hardly wetting skin and hair when it vanished.

Archer's had stopped and started ten times by now.

"Need the soap," I told him.

Another few minutes before he passed it over at the top of the door and I found it with groping fingers.

The stuff stank with some nasty fake perfume. The bottle was squat and slick. I dropped it twice and had to hunt for it on the floor, again feeling over a lifetime of who knew what all along that floor. I didn't care how much they cleaned. I wouldn't have wanted to drag my hands around inside a clean toilet either.

All while the water was off, of course. I tried feebly to restart it a couple of times but again could not find the nob.

Soaked and frozen, part soaped and wishing I had never started, furious with Archer for dumping me, I spent minutes chasing the bottle, then setting it on the floor in a corner where I could find it and hunting for the knob. Now, I kept one hand on it while I tried to turn and scrub and rinse at the same time, pushing that damn thing over and over as each spray lasted about twenty seconds—which felt like two.

I never warmed up. I never really finished rinsing off. I finally settled, let the thing stay off, and reached for the towel I had draped over the door.

"Archer? Did you move my towel?"

"No." He was drying off beside my stall, his own shower having stopped minutes before.

I felt down the door, into the open air below it, and on to the floor. There was my towel. It must have slid off the far side of the little half door because only about a third of it was soaked and dripping with shower water. The remainder was lying in a wad on the public bathroom floor.

Silently, I started to pat dry, rubbed my hair back and forth, but soon could not stand it and reached from my flapping door to the window ledge just beyond where I had mashed my jeans and clean underwear from my carry-on into a ball for safekeeping.

Shaking, dripping, and covered in goose bumps, I pulled on only the jeans to keep the underwear dry, and hurried out. I had no idea how many doors to count to find ours, so had to wait for Archer to escort me into the hall.

"What happened to your towel?" he asked.

"What do you think? It was left in the care of a blind guy."

"We weren't going to shower together—"

"It was empty. It's still empty. It was empty the whole damn time. Even if it was Grand Central, I didn't know you'd just dump me in there. Where's the room? I've got to get these off to dry."

"What do you want, Noah?" Leading us, Archer's voice was no longer angry, like my own. He sounded tired.

What the hell did he think I wanted after I'd already twice spelled it out?

I said nothing as I felt my way into the room, along a shelf, to the foot of a twin bed with a cheap metal frame, along that to our bags, then a pillowcase I removed for some effort to dry myself.

I heard Archer move around, finishing dressing himself in the travel clothes from the day before. Popping sound of a pen, probably as he made a list of stuff we needed.

It wasn't until he said he was going downstairs to see if they had anything for us to eat or find out about a nearby breakfast option that I felt bad about being testy with him. If walking barefoot in those showers and bathroom floor bothered me, it must have made Archer want to scrub his own feet with steel wool and antiseptic. And it wasn't his fault I dropped my towel. You didn't need sight to be able to hang something carefully. I would have been just as likely to drop it eight years ago. Although, if he had been willing to share with me, he would have caught it.

I found my cane where I'd left it the previous night on the foot of the second bed, dressed the rest of the way, though it took some time even to find my shoes, then felt back with the cane to the built-in shelves along a wall. All the way to the door, I found my jacket hanging up and dry, where Archer must have left it for me.

I pulled this on, assuring myself of phone and passport and wallet. Archer had tried to convince me to wear a money belt and be more careful with my stuff. Maybe a blind guy was a bit of a target for pickpockets, but I had enough trouble dealing with everything else about travel without adding new, inaccessible and impossible-to-keep-track-of accessories.

I normally never carried cash with me at home, debiting everything and entering a PIN on a Braille keypad. But we'd had to get hundreds of dollars in cash changed to euros before we left because we hadn't wanted to be faced with all those overseas card charges.

I loved the new bills. Each one a slightly different size. You could actually feel what note you held. For the first time in years, I could tell if I was paying someone with a five or a twenty. For the first time in years, I felt free to carry cash. As to why US bills were not varied sizes to allow for diversity among their users, I was still drawing a blank.

Pulled together, with my belongings back on my person, I scoped out the rest of the room with cane and fingers. A heavy, automatically locking door, like any hotel room door, was in the center of a narrow wall. Feeling this, the room's width was only about seven feet.

From this door, if you walked straight in, you could walk straight out. That is, there was a pathway to a large window, which Archer had left cracked open despite the chill autumn. More claustrophobia issues.

When you first stepped in through the doorway, there were simple board shelves fixed right onto the wall with steel brackets. No back or sides to the shelves. Just wall. To the left was a small table and two chairs, plastic and aluminum or some other metal, it seemed. By the table was the foot of one bed, with the foot of the other by the shelves. The window was between and above the two heads of the little beds. There was not much more than a foot of space between the two.

From door to window was no more than eleven or twelve feet.

Out in the hall, voices, steps, and opening and shutting doors grew noticeable.

I asked my phone for the time by unlocking the screen and tapping the top right corner for the voice-over to read *7:50 a.m.*

I removed my laptop from my bag and set it up on the table, turning it on. Archer wouldn't travel with one—even been surprised I insisted I needed mine. But Archer was not dependent on his tactile keyboard interface and speech-to-text/text-to-speech software, which I relied upon on a daily basis. He also had no ambitions of continuing work on his new comic book project while on this trip.

First technology snag—Internet password. We had it printed on something somewhere in the room. The Dutch had considerate currency. They probably did not have their hostel WiFi passwords in Braille.

I opened my file of notes on my newly blossoming comic masterpiece, adding Archer's two cents from the day before.

Footsteps in the hall, key card sliding in the lock, and the door opened.

"Hey," Archer said. "Get online?"

"Very funny." I closed the laptop, remembering again snapping at him and not wanting him to think I didn't care about him coming back. "This room is tiny."

"Yeah, I noticed."

"I smell coffee."

"I brought some breakfast back. There's way more food than I was expecting for a hostel. I talked to a guy down there about places to shop for shampoo and shirts around here, so that's what kept me."

"No problem." Remaining at the table, I moved my laptop to the foot of the bed behind me, feeling over the metal frame. "Sit down. What'd you bring?"

"One big coffee mug to share and one heaped plate to share." Shifting, setting down heavy, ceramic sounds, not paper. "I wasn't sure I could manage more on all those stairs."

"I never knew how spoiled we are with elevators in America."

Archer laughed as he sat. "They have elevators in the Netherlands, Noah. We're just in a really old place with a low budget."

"What color is the tabletop?"

"Red plastic. And the bed frames are painted red metal. And the door is red. Walls light gray. Shelves are wood and I think the floor is fake wood."

"At least there's no carpet," I said. "All the carpet in hotels at home is gross."

"That's putting it mildly. Here." Archer's warm fingertips stroked the back of my hand and I lifted my right to move with his and feel the heavy mug. "It's cool enough to drink."

That faint, gentle touch, exactly what I needed from him to find my way, exactly who I loved so much, made me remember why we were here.

"I'm sorry we're starting our honeymoon off with such a...bang," I said, lifting the mug. "Not your dream trip after all."

"We'll figure it out. Just got here. We have eight nights to go and it's all improving from here, right?"

"Right." I smiled, wishing his hand was on mine again. Or we were back in bed. So much for the first night of the honeymoon.

The coffee was strong and bitter. I greatly preferred a latte, but this morning, I needed it. Archer also had thick slices of a sweet, moist spice cake, much like gingerbread, which were lathered with butter, soft and hard sliced cheeses, cold cuts, and fresh whole grain bread with sunflower seeds.

"Try this." We had been through most of the plate when Archer drew my hand to a slice of bread, spread thickly in something that was sticky when my finger brushed it.

Imagining peanut butter, I lifted the slice and took a bite. I almost spat it out, not because it was bad, but from the shock

"What—?" I coughed and swallowed. "Is that chocolate frosting?"

Archer laughed. "Chocolate spread. The guy downstairs assured me he ate chocolate spread on white bread every morning for breakfast growing up."

"Not bad, I guess. What's up with all the starch and sugar, though? This is like an American diet. I thought people weren't obese over here."

"That's a gross generalization, but now that you mention it, I don't remember seeing anyone dangerously overweight since we got to the city. And did you know the Dutch, as a people, are the tallest in the world?"

"Are you saying chocolate spread and white bread are building better bodies?"

"Makes you wonder," Archer said. "They also have all this protein in their breakfasts, though. Hard to imagine this for breakfast at an American hotel. They still have nothing but various forms of processed carbs and sugar and fruit."

"I wouldn't say no to an orange." I loved oranges and grapefruits. I'd rather eat an orange than chocolate chip cookies, even as a kid.

"Well, now..." Archer shifted, jacket rustling.

I reached out eagerly with my left hand and Archer placed a warm, slightly tacky orb in my palm.

"They had a basket of them. Totally random. There was no other fruit."

"They knew I was coming." I passed him back half the slice with chocolate spread.

"I guess so. Happy honeymoon."

"Happy honeymoon, Archer. Can we make a toast to us and our new lives together even though we're sharing a mug?"

"You could drink your orange. But better save it for later since we have this spice cake to finish."

I set down the orange and lifted the mug. "To us. And Amsterdam. May the rest of the trip progress better than the start."

"A bit cynical, but a good sentiment, I guess."

I drank. "You've got some nerve calling me cynical." And passed him the mug.

"I'm practical, Noah. I've always been practical. You're the one who fluctuates between morbid pessimism and weirdly naïve optimism. Often throwing in a spoonful of self-pity."

"I have a lot of challenges to overcome."

"So you've told me." With a bit of a snort. Which was so, so uncalled for. Especially after the morning I'd had. Why was he always acting like I was perfectly fine? I wanted other people to act like I was perfectly fine. Not Archer. Archer should treat me with...well...dignity. Care and respect for my situation.

"Now what's wrong?" Archer asked.

I must have recoiled a bit at his words. "Nothing."

"And?" Archer prompted.

I didn't answer for a moment, then, quickly, "You say you're practical, but you're not practical about me. You act like there's nothing wrong and you can just dump me in a strange shower situation like that and I'll be fine. Then you say I'm the one with an attitude problem. A practical person would have helped out a bit, don't you think?"

"I'm sorry you're upset about the shower." Though his tone was rather cold. "And no, I don't think that. I happen to know you are extremely capable and also extremely irritable about anyone 'helping' you 'too much.' How many showers have you taken alone in your life? Thousands—"

"Not here."

"You knew what the situation would be before we came. Private room, shared bath—"

"I didn't think about you freaking out at even the prospect of someone maybe, possibly, coming into the bathroom at the same time you were in a shower stall with me—even in off hours and with somewhat private showers.

Which I should have, obviously, because you've always been like that. No reason marriage or maternity or anything like that should matter."

Silence. Then Archer spoke slowly. "Did you mean 'modernity'?"

"That's what I said." Snapping at him.

"No, you said 'maternity.' Which is not exactly—"

"Whatever. You knew what I meant."

"Actually, I had to think about it. But okay. I'm sorry you're upset. I'm sorry we couldn't book a five-star hotel room with a private, accessible bathroom and a TV you could talk to and twenty-four/seven room service to look after you whenever I was falling down on the job. I thought you knew what we were getting into and I thought you wanted to be here."

I turned my head away, eyes shut, hand on the orange on the table before me. The chair felt very stiff all of a sudden. The room very quiet. Also frigid with the window open and...other elements floating around.

I should have apologized. Archer hated being poor. He worked really hard and we were doing better and this was a dream. And I was kicking it into the sand for him. He was right that I would get angry over him looking after me too much. And it was true that he usually did *not* look after me too much. Just exactly enough.

He knew how to help me get around and when I needed extra—like guiding my hand to the plate with the lightest touch. He described views and colors and situations for me without being asked. He knew what was important to me, and what didn't matter and what I could do for myself. You couldn't teach someone the little things that Archer understood on his own about what I needed from him. You couldn't manufacture that detail, the thought and love in his gestures. And couldn't replace it.

Archer set down the mug, shifting the plate. Silence growing longer.

I swallowed, shivering a little. "Sorry."

Archer said nothing.

"I don't need fancy hotels. I don't even care about that stuff. And I know you don't. This is fine. I don't want to argue with you for the whole trip."

"Then don't, Noah." His tone remained terse. He stood up and walked across the tiny room, between the beds. I thought he was going to get something, but heard the window shut instead. He walked back to his chair. "You'd be surprised how easy it is not to. It might actually even take *less* effort than arguing all the time, believe it or not. I guess you'd lose a lot of meaning in your life without a good daily argument, though."

"I don't mean to be so argumentative."

"Don't you mean 'augmentative'?"

"What? No..." I turned my head, watching his voice again. Archer looked at me when he talked to me. A lot of people didn't. I could always tell. "That wasn't wrong."

"No." He chuckled a little. "Not that time. I was just messing with you. I'll go over the shower with you tonight, both dressed, make sure you know where everything is and have a safe place for your towel, okay? It was tough even for me to use, but I think I get the system now."

"Okay." I turned my face down to my orange. "Thanks, Archer. You can make a toast also. If you want to..." I bit my lip.

"Oh, I don't know." He picked up something from the plate, chewed a moment, then lifted either the plate or mug. "To the years ahead—the lifetime after the honeymoon. Here."

He passed me the mug and I drank. I still didn't like the coffee. But sharing it with him made all the difference.

Chapter Eight

ARCHER ASSURED ME we were staying in the heart of Amsterdam's best shopping district. This accommodation had been all about location and price. We could put up with a party hostel for everything else.

The trouble was twofold—the price tag accompanying the best shopping in Amsterdam, and the types of shops being inappropriate to what we were after. Oh, yes, and most happened to be closed at 8:00 a.m. on a Saturday morning. We wanted a Walgreens, or, better yet, Target. We had a Coach and Prada and some of the highest-end fashion and leather goods on the planet.

Nice shopping with you.

First thing on a Saturday morning, we could both breathe easy on the streets themselves. Archer talked softly about the stunning architecture, which enchanted him, the misty canals, and autumn colors appearing in not only trees throughout the park across from our accommodations but in small trees dotted across the city.

We, at last, found an open store, which he described as a very small Safeway—a brand-name, cheap grocery store with toiletries and greeting cards and magazines. The place was quiet and hummed with electric currents of all grocery stores, scattered with a few shoppers.

Archer picked out toothpaste and a toothbrush for himself, disposable razors, then soap and shampoo that he assured me had rabbit symbols on the backs—not animal tested.

Checking out, he got a recommendation—for the first time in faltering English—for a place to try for clothes. It was finally 10:00 a.m. by then and we spent a solid half hour trying to find the store while the streets grew crowded.

Once we did reach them, Archer was traumatized by the prices.

With the exchange rate, we were facing cheap, sweatshop T-shirts from China for $40 and up. Underwear $10 and up. Each. No discount three- or six-packs like a box store at home. The socks actually made him gasp. He didn't even say anything about their prices.

"Should we try somewhere else?" I asked, fingering a display of hanging socks he had led us to. Not as if they were SmartWool either. Just a cheap poly-cotton elastic blend. I could always tell fabrics by feel.

Archer sighed. "Where? There's nothing like this out here. We're so screwed."

"We'll skip eating for a day or two and be square."

"More like a week."

"Let's go back to the grocery store and get some bread and...chocolate spread or whatever—carrots, cheese, I don't know—and eat that for a couple lunches. We can't just not buy this stuff. We can't even do laundry."

I noticed he hadn't mentioned pants and decided I wouldn't either. We could wear the same jeans until they were walking around on their own as long as we showered and otherwise changed. The rest of this stuff...we kind of needed.

"I'm sorry," he muttered. "Not how—"

"This isn't your fault. Shit happens, Archer. Don't I know."

He said nothing for a moment but let out another breath.

"Just a few things," I said. "Then a couple of groceries. Maybe we'll find another place. And maybe laundry also. I could stay in bed, working on my epic, while you find a laundromat for one of our outfits at a time."

Archer chuckled a little.

"Hell, if we bought baking soda and vinegar, we could wash stuff in the sink," I went on. "Think of it as camping."

"Sure. You know how much I love to camp, Noah."

"There's the spirits."

"Where are they? I need some."

I laughed. "You know what I mean."

"*That's the spirit*? I don't think you realize how dramatically these slight differences can change what you—"

"I always know what I'm talking about. I'm an expat."

"You mean an—?" He stopped himself, tone changing now. "Sometimes, I don't know. I used to think it was always an honest mistake. But now...are you just trying to see if I'm paying attention? Is it laziness? I know you know the difference between an expert and an expat."

"Did I tell you I looked up 'column' this morning?" I asked. "Turns out, it has multiple meanings, like so many English words, and they are not all vertical."

"I didn't realize you ever bothered looking words up. No reason to quit winging it now. Red, black, or green?" He was pushing a poly-cotton shirt into my hands.

"Black."

"Hmm." He pulled one shirt away and gave me another. "Maybe we should both wear red and yellow to help the bicyclists see us."

"Based on experiences so far, I'd say the bikers around here don't give a shit if they see us or not. They'll just keep doing what they're doing, and if we don't get out of the way, it's our funeral."

"That's true." I could tell Archer had his back to me, presumably picking out a shirt for himself. "And we'll have jackets on the whole time we're here anyway so not going to matter so much about the shirts."

"I told you I wanted black."

"You're holding black." He still spoke to me while facing away.

"I am not."

There was a pause. Archer turned to me. "How do you know that?"

A test. *I knew it.*

"Why don't you believe me when I say I can tell certain colors?" I asked.

"Because it's impossible. You don't know what color that shirt is."

"It's red." I held it up.

Silence.

He snatched it back from me. "You're guessing."

"Whatever. Give me a black one."

"Pick one out for yourself, since you know so much."

"Archer."

He pressed another shirt into my hands. I was pretty sure it was black.

"Thank you."

"You freak me out sometimes, Noah." His back was to me again, choosing his own shirt.

"That shouldn't really be my problem." I felt over the shirt, checking for graphics or patterns. "What's this?"

"It's got a gray outline of local canal houses on the chest. It's stylized. You'd like it."

That sounded acceptable. I ran my fingertips over the different texture of the gray.

"Okay, I've got a red one with a bird on it. Raven maybe," Archer said. "Want to feel that?"

"Yes." I took the second shirt.

"Let's get a couple pairs of underwear and get out of here before I have a premature heart attack."

"That would certainly leave me in a pickle," I said absently as I examined his shirt.

"Your concern is touching." Archer sighed.

"You're not going to have a heart attack. We're fine."

Out of the little clothing outlet, or whatever it was—felt like an outlet—we did return to the grocery place for a few items.

Again on narrow sidewalk, I held Archer's arm and my cane while he carried our bags, saying almost nothing about the sights now as we made our way back to the hostel. By this hour of the morning, getting close to lunch, the sidewalks were packed. We had another round of starting, stopping, Archer yanking me aside by the hand on his arm, turns without warning, pedestrians constantly brushing past us—left, right, near misses—ringing of bike bells, and voices in Dutch coming from all directions.

Sun out now. I could feel it on my face and was glad I had gone with the dark glasses today. Glad I thought to put them in my carry-on with my toothbrush and not in the checked bag with my whole wardrobe for a nine-day trip.

Archer was panting by the time we reached Uptown Vondelpark Hostel. Six steps, door, into a lobby—now quiet. Just a few voices in French perhaps. No more.

Archer started ahead and to the left while I counted my steps to the foot of all those stairs. There was a door first that he had to use his key card to get through.

He'd just slid it in place and I was feeling the height and type of the door handle myself, when a man's voice some way to our right said, "Archer Lucassen? Were you expecting a call?"

Archer whipped around, myself still holding the cold leaver knob, heart leaping.

"From the airport?" Archer asked.

"You just missed them," the guy said, cheery tone, smiling. "They said they have a bag of yours at baggage claim and will drop it off here sometime tomorrow."

"Thank you. Wonderful, thank you so much. Any idea how late they will be there? We'll go ahead and get it ourselves."

"Probably not past seventeen hundred. I would go as soon as possible if you want it today."

I had to calculate that in my head, knowing only that 1:00 p.m. was 13:00, as we climbed the stairs.

"Another trip to the airport," I said, grinning. "And just when we were getting used to this city."

"Anything. It's worth it to get it tonight. I'm glad we didn't buy more."

In the room, Archer was quick to dump everything and say there wasn't a moment to spare. Who knew how long it would take to get back and find the right people?

"What about lunch?" I asked. "I haven't even washed my hands. We need a minute."

"We have bread, peanut butter, bananas, cheese, and bottled water. I'll make us sandwiches."

Archer was impatient about the empty bathrooms and my insisting he remain with me to return to our own room. I couldn't even remember my step count yet.

He made us peanut butter sandwiches with seedy bread while I ate Baby Bell cheeses. I could have my orange for dessert if I wasn't rushed out of there like the place was on fire.

"It's okay, Archer." He was already pushing a sandwich into my hand as I peeled off a second cheese wax.

I wondered if we should let the airport drivers bring our bag to the hostel, as they were apparently planning. Archer did not seem to be in a deterrable mood, however.

He spoke with his mouth full. "I'm not taking any chances with these people being there. The sooner we go, the better. Find the person who called. It's a Saturday. We're lucky they called at all. Bet they tried my phone and it didn't work—or just didn't want to mess with that number." Gulping and twisting a cap off a water bottle in front of my face where I sat at the table.

I could predict problems ahead.

Did he think I was going to "run" to the tram back to the train station? What about those midday Saturday crowds exploding on those rough, jagged sidewalks as we spoke?

"Archer—?"

"Does this taste funny to you?"

I hadn't even tried mine but took a bite of the peanut butter sandwich. "No." I chewed more. "Yeah. Shit. That stuff's turned."

"That's what I was afraid of." Mouth full again. "Tastes a little rancid."

"It's totally rancid." I held mine back out in the general direction of above the table. "Scrape it off. I'll just eat the bread with cheese."

"You need more than that."

"I'll get my daily caloric intake up with our steak and lobster dinner," I said.

Gulping, he took the sandwich from me. At home, he would have told me to do it myself—I wasn't an invalid. But I didn't even know what he was using for utensils. He must have kept a fork and butter knife from downstairs this morning. Or, he was in such a hurry, maybe he was slapping the peanut butter on with his fingers. That wouldn't be Archer's style, though. Something I would do.

"We got a chunk of supposedly Dutch cheese also. I'll slice that on there." He gave me back a cheese sandwich with only hints of rancid peanut still about it.

"You shouldn't eat that." I could tell he was finishing off his own sandwich. "Isn't that like eating mold or something?"

"It's what we've got."

Usually he was the cautious one. But he also had tunnel vision when he needed to get something done. Archer was a straight-A student.

"Come on. Just bring that with you." Scrape of his chair.

"You're losing it. You want me to walk, hold onto you, hold the cane, eat a sandwich, and not die on the street in this crazy city? All at once?"

"Then hurry up." Sound of him zipping his jacket.

I gulped. Archer rustled around me, dropping stuff on the table, rummaging in his bag behind and to my right at the second bed.

"I'll take the boarding pass. It has the bag stub on it for the receipt."

"I still can't believe they called," I said. "What do you think happened?"

"Who knows? Come on."

"God, Archer." I pushed back my own chair but still had half a sandwich. "Did you taste that Dutch cheese? Really good."

"Uh-huh. Noah...?" Voice by the door now. Probably had his hand on the knob. I could almost hear him tapping his toe.

"I'm coming. I'm coming." I stood, feeling for the cane lying on the table.

"Are you sure...?" Archer continued. "You want to go?"

"What?"

"I mean...if you want to. But...why are you coming back to the airport? It took forever to get out here. And I know you were wanting to work on your computer."

I pushed the last corner of the sandwich into my mouth, looped the cane handle on my wrist, and thought about that.

"You don't have to," Archer said. "I could be back in a few hours unless the trains are just really spread out. Dinnertime at the latest. You know how to get to and from the bathroom and stairs. There's always someone at the front desk if anything comes up."

He was trying to get rid of me. But what bothered me was why I hadn't thought to volunteer this option. Obviously, Archer did not need to take me with him back to the airport to collect our bag. And how, exactly, would he get the rolling bag here with both it and me to keep up with on the return? On a Saturday evening in those ridiculous packed streets?

"Yeah," I said before he had to feel any worse about it. "I don't even know why I was thinking I should come. That's...kind of stupid. You go, rescue our wardrobe, and I'll take you to dinner when you get back. With my very own, usable cash."

"Are you sure, though? If you're not comfortable staying—"

"No. I'm really, really sure. That's the best idea you've had all trip. I'm going to either work on this comic outline or fall into a jet-lag-induced coma, but I'm sure I don't need to go back to the airport."

"Okay." Voice closer, stepping toward me as he spoke. "Sorry, Noah. Crazy couple of days."

"We'll start fresh tomorrow." I smiled. "Briefs, shampoo, shaving, and all."

He kissed me, only slightly startling me since I heard and felt him step up to me. His lips tasted like that nasty peanut butter, and I laughed.

"Don't eat any more of that garbage."

"I'll be right back. You're sure?"

"Go on. I'll be here. Miss you. Love you."

"I love you. See you for dinner." Bounding away again, pulling open the door.

"*Archer*, wait. WiFi password?"

He laughed. "Oh, right."

Scene Two

CHRIS BOWYER OPENS the door to allow his guide dog to leap from the car on command. He follows, leather handle and leash in his left hand. As the door shuts behind him, Robert Perth's voice comes from somewhere ahead and to his right.

"Devil, forward," Chris says and the handle pulls against his fingers as the German shepherd dog strides off.

Two steps of frosty grass crunch below his shoes along the curb where he climbed out, then hard, unyielding cement of a sidewalk.

Devil hesitates in the harness.

"Devil, right."

The dog moves on, and Chris turns his head as the voices change from forward and right to forward and left.

"Chris. There he is. Chris, up here, you're right at the footpath." The calling comes from Perth, nearby now.

"Devil, left." Broken cement walkway up to the house itself, presumably.

Perth's heavy footfalls thump down three wooden steps, then hit the cement before him.

Chris stops. Devil waits.

"Ready for this one?"

"Is it Whiteout?" Chris asks.

"Same neighborhood, same MO, same pattern in everything. You tell me."

"Is it taped?"

"Not for you. Come on."

Chris tells his dog to go. Devil pauses to indicate the first step, then all three of them walk up to a creaking, uneven porch, which sags below Chris's feet, sinking in the middle at the door—assuming the door is opposite those few steps.

Perth confirms this. "Door's open. It'll take you into a foyer facing a hall to the kitchen. Right's the living room, left's a bedroom. The place is tiny. Like a one-bedroom apartment in Manhattan. One story. Don't know why, or how, they got all these victims in here."

Chris smells mold and dry rot, rust, faint hints of cigarette smoke and cat's urine from months or years back.

He steps onto a threadbare rug. Another step and a wood floor creaks.

Police radios and voices fade as he turns to his left and relaxes the steel hold he usually keeps in place, exposing his own mind.

He sees a dozen women sitting tightly squeezed into two dilapidated couches and a few chairs. Each face is flushed, glassy-eyed. They wear short cocktail dresses and heels, earrings and lipstick and eyeliner. Each holds a shot glass in one hand, each sitting up straight and still, breathing fast, breasts rising and falling below low-cut polyester of sky blue and red, salmon, pink, and moss green.

"Talk to me," Perth says behind him.

Chris turns his head, looking into the long, narrow kitchen at the back of the house, out through the back windows to a tiny yard of weeds—and a broken fence being struck repeatedly with a sledgehammer, breaking down sections. He takes another step to see the man swinging the hammer, how the sun blazes down on his tool belt and safety helmet, how yellow dandelions bloom all over the yard.

"Is there a fence out back?" Chris asks.

"Yes. Old wood one."

So that part was in the future. Perth would not care about a construction worker leveling the fence in some future summer. Perth was not nearly as interested in the future as he should be. He cared about the past.

"Women this time," Chris says.

"Yes."

"You said everything was the same."

"Everything but that. Just like the last place except chicks instead of guys."

"You think Whiteout is bisexual?"

"Very funny, Chris. Cut the crap. What'd you see?"

"Thirteen women in here, all in cocktail dresses and heels. Chief, this wasn't Whiteout."

"What? You saw someone with them?"

"No. But I'm sure it wasn't. They had glasses for drinks. Whiteout uses injections. They were all dressed. Whiteout strips his followers. They were all together as thirteen. Whiteout keeps one back. It wasn't him. It was an imitator."

"Jesus Christ," Perth whispers behind him. "We can't deal with two of these assholes right now."

Chris's phone rings and he reaches into his pocket, left hand still on Devil's harness and lead.

He does not ask for the audio caller ID with Perth standing there. "Hello?"

"Hey, Chris. Really sorry to bother you."

"It's okay, Trent. What's wrong?"

"There's been, uh, sort of emergency. You don't think...you can...get home soon, do you?"

"What happened?" Chris asks.

"Just...soon as you can. I don't—oh, shit! Got to go! Come home!"

The connection goes dead.

Heart pounding, Chris drops the phone back in his pocket. "Sorry, Chief. Emergency."

"What's up? We need your help on this, Chris."

"I'll come back, see if I can get more. Devil, left, door, forward. All I can tell you right now is it wasn't Whiteout. There were thirteen bodies, right? Identical?"

"Right."

"Something else he doesn't do. Leaving the thirteenth with the rest? And no mess? But these were the same. It's an imitator."

"Don't walk out. You just got here."

Chris is already down the three steps with Devil, back to the broken cement path. "Hire me onto your force with a living wage and super benefits and I'll stay around when you tell me, Chief. When you call in favors, you get what you pay for. But thanks for your concern about the emergency."

"You don't call this a fucking emergency?" shouting behind him.

"Devil, car." Chris feels his way back to the frosted grass, reaching, noting Devil pause, window glass, then the door handle. He pulls it open, the two climb in, and Chris asks Ethan to drive home while Perth is still calling and sputtering back on the sidewalk.

Chapter Nine

"TO BEING BACK on track." Archer toasted us with great enthusiasm this time.

I lifted my glass for him to touch mine. "To an awesome honeymoon in Amsterdam."

"I can't believe we're really here. First day a fail, but that's why we stayed for as long as we could, right?" He was still happy, sounding almost giddy following his afternoon's adventure.

I had no idea how he managed. I thought I'd write half a dozen scenes after he left me in the room. I'd finished one before I fell asleep in a jet-lagged stupor. Barely even that much. I had totally lied to Archer when he woke me up an hour ago, telling him I must have just dozed off.

Now I was making good on my promise to take him to dinner. A real traditional Dutch place that Archer had on his list weeks ago.

We started with water—the food cost enough and we'd known we wouldn't be drinking on this trip—and a soup called *snert*—yum—served with rye bread and bacon bits on top. Then celery root and potato *stamppot* with sausage and gravy. The whole thing was rather textureless, but hot and fabulous after eating a couple slices of bread and cheese for lunch.

I couldn't wait to share my comic outline progress with Archer, but I asked him about his trip to the airport instead and we talked about the food and the city and everything he wanted to see. People throw that word around a lot, even Archer. It's meaningless to them.

I made myself wait until after dinner and back in the room. Then Archer had to "put away" and "clean up." Like we were at home. Like it made a difference. We were living out of a suitcase, which we were lucky to have, for a week in a tiny room with two shelves and a table. What could he possibly clean up?

But I kept mum and busied myself with emails, then had a beeping warning from Skype. Shiloh calling. It was morning her time.

We talked for fifteen minutes and Archer came over to where I was sitting on the bed to say hi, but the connection was horrible. She kept cutting off and coming back. I didn't even mention the lost bag, just asked about my dog and said we were fine.

Luath, my white golden retriever, had not been parted from me since we first met at the service dog training facility in California. I asked Shiloh to take some pictures and email her puppy raisers as long as she was there. Archer did this for me now and then and I tried to stay in touch with the family, but I wasn't much of a photographer these days.

She told me Luath kept waiting by the door, where she had last seen me walking out with Archer a couple mornings ago. Of course, that made me feel rotten and I wished she hadn't.

"Mom made vegetarian chili yesterday and it wasn't half bad," Shiloh told me next while I was still trying to tell her what to do to comfort Luath. "Especially with cheese and sour cream. I don't know what I'll do if she goes vegan."

Shiloh was still living at home and they took turns cooking. Mom had gone more and more vegetarian on us over the past five years and finally written off meat, fish, and eggs altogether, saying the consumption of meat the way it was being produced in the world today was destroying the planet. This was probably true. But I noticed she still drove a car and bought new clothes. Aren't those things destroying the world as well?

When I first started shopping around for telephone jobs as I was losing my sight, I'd worked for an environmental nonprofit. Ten minutes with them and I was pretty sure everything I did, every move I made, every word I said, and yes, every thought I had, was contributing to the annihilation of Earth.

Mom says I'm avoiding the issue—that our food industry is worse than almost anything and that we all must start somewhere. But I don't live at home anymore. I married an omnivore. And I've never had chili without at least a little turkey in it.

"You need to get Luath out more," I told Shiloh. "Get her mind on something else. Harness her and pretend she's working."

Shiloh knew Luath's commands.

"I get it, Noah. She's out—" Broken up. Nothing. "—the time with—" Nothing, nothing, nothing. "—anymore."

"I've got to go," I said. "The hostel connection sucks."

"Who—?" Nothing. "—hostel—"

"Sorry, Shiloh. Take care of Luath. I'll call you later. Tell Mom I said hi."

"—for their honeymoon?"

"Sue us. It was cheap. You can go rent out Windsor Castle when you get married if you want. See if we care. Good night—or whatever time it is."

"Good night, Noah! Bye, Archer!" Shouting then, like that would help the connection.

"Thanks for calling for a dog update, Shiloh," Archer said. "We appreciate you watching her."

Archer thought I was rude and he needed to set an example. Like a bratty kid. Shiloh was crazy about him. When we were all teens, she could hardly be in the room with him, flushed and avoiding eye contact if he came over, making an extra effort to wear her oldest jeans and weirdest vintage tops from Mom's art shows. Now, she would appreciate him thanking her more than she would me thanking her anyway. And I was still too upset about Luath's suffering for much gratitude.

With the laptop closed, I asked Archer what he thought about my dog pining away.

"Shiloh will take her out to the dog park or something fun that she doesn't often get to do. That will distract her," Archer said, stepping back and forth by me at the bed, moving and folding and cleaning. Whatever that meant in context.

"She doesn't live by a good dog park. Luath doesn't care about a bunch of strangers anyway."

"Uh...she kind of does, Noah. You and her are both extroverts. Come here."

"That doesn't mean we're not loyal to our own." I stood unwillingly from the bed, feeling the foot to step toward him between shelves and table.

"Loyalty to loved ones doesn't mean you can't run around a wet park now and then with a springer spaniel. Look at this." He took my hand and pulled it to feel a shelf so I could "look." "All your clothes stacked on this one, okay? Socks, underwear, shirts, pants, in that order. My stuff is on the one above, my towel and a fresh one for you are hanging from the top shelf. The bag's under the bed, out of the way. All the shower and bathroom stuff is on the table at the back, against the wall. All the food is at the front of the table right behind you. Our backpacks are still on the extra bed, your stuff toward the head, mine toward the foot."

"Shower flip-flops?" I asked.

"Yours are by the door."

I turned, as if to the door, and caught his arm instead. I could almost always find the rest of a person from the sound of a voice.

"I don't deserve you." I ducked my head against his shoulder, hugging him.

"So I've heard, Noah. Then you turn around and call me names. Speaking of loyalty."

"I'm sorry." I chuckled and kissed his neck, which he does not like. He was always weird about his neck, but I could not see him any other way than touch, so he let me poke him. For the most part.

"Stop it." He turned slightly, twisting away. "What did you get done today while I was gone? Besides sleep for most of the afternoon?"

"I did not. I had just dozed off." I lifted my face to find his lips.

"I bet you had." He returned my kiss, reaching to push his fingers through my hair with both hands.

His mouth tasted of his reclaimed toothpaste, mint and baking soda. He had brushed his teeth for about ten minutes after he got his toothbrush back. And another round after our Dutch dinner. He pressed against me, pushing my head back, taking me by surprise. I couldn't let him get carried away. Not when he had finally asked about my afternoon's masterpiece.

"I wrote," I said, a bit breathless as I turned my face and dropped my head once more. "I'm working on the comic idea."

"Quit it." My nose had hardly touched skin of his throat when he pushed me away. "You don't have to be such a vampire."

"You know, a lot of people enjoy an erotic kiss on the neck."

"You should have married one of them and you two could have at it," Archer said.

"I wrote the next scene, announcing the hero."

"You mean *introducing*?"

"And I'd love for you to tell me what you think."

Archer sighed, shoving me back from kissing him.

I grabbed his arm so he could not skulk and stepped with him to the bed. Archer was almost as good a skulker as a sigher.

"Aren't you rushing the feedback thing?" He sat on the little bed, me following, scrambling onto it on my knees beside him. "Don't you need to get a first draft written, or at least half the treatment? Then we can discuss it?"

"That's just silly. You're right here. I want to know what you think. Then I know what to work on the first time around. It will only take you a minute to read." I touched his hair with my nose, kissed his ear, and wrapped my arms around him. "Please. The laptop's there at the head of the bed."

"I know. I can see it."

"You're so arrogant," I said. "Don't be a dickhead again."

"I thought we decided I wasn't one in the first place."

"You are when you want to be. So smug about your beautiful eyes."

Archer laughed. "We're supposed to live grateful lives, right? So I have an attitude of gratitude about my eyes." He kissed me, hands on my face again, blocking off words.

I twisted away. "Read for me? Please? There could be a blowjob in it for you."

"Right." Still chuckling, still touching me. "And if I don't read for you, there won't be? Is that what you're implying?"

I didn't have an argument for that. "If you'll read first and tell me what you think, I won't touch your neck."

That one apparently got him thinking.

I leaned in to kiss him while he hesitated, finding his lips, his nose, his eyelids.

"What do you want me to read?" He ran his hands down my chest.

"It should still be there on the screen. Just close Skype or whatever's on." I ruffled his hair and pushed him toward the head of the bed and the laptop.

"Whatever's on? You don't know what's open on your laptop?" Archer leaned over, making the bed shift. "Must have been housekeeping on that porn site. Wait, there is no housekeeping. We're staying in a hostel."

"You're worse and worse. What use could I have for a porn site? Think I want to hear people groan? That's the most visual of all visual arts."

"Porn stories? Your screenreader could read it to you."

"I'm sure it'd be hot in the flat monotone she uses." I was the one almost sighing then. "Go on and read. I'll practice a trip to the bathroom counting steps and brush my teeth and try to feel like a normal person."

"You cannot possibly have ever felt like a normal person in your life, Noah. Unless you're even better at deluding yourself than I thought. Okay, there it is. Go test the bathroom journey, and if you're not back in an hour, I'll come looking for you."

"An hour? How about ten minutes?"

He was chuckling again as I crossed to the door, finding my cane. "And don't forget your promise."

"About the blowjob?"

"About my neck."

"Oh, yeah. I forgot."

"Very funny."

Making my way to the bathroom, I frittered about as much as I could. Some guys in the halls, someone just coming out of one of the bathrooms as I got there. A woman calling through a door in Dutch down the hall. Doors opening and shutting.

Not a lot of excitement, though. I carefully counted and felt doors, holding my breath wondering if I was trying to get into the wrong room with my card. Had I gone too far? One door too many? No, all good.

Archer said nothing when I returned. He would be reading.

Too early to get ready for bed? It felt like 1:00 a.m.

I reached for my phone in my little heap of possessions on the spare bed, but Archer must have noticed.

"It's past eight," he said. "Long since dark out."

"Close enough to go to bed then," I said, sitting down to pull off shoes and socks. "We'll feel better about the time zone in the morning."

He said nothing, must have been back to reading, and I took my time about undressing and folding my clothes onto the spare bed by my pack. Were we moving the bed over? I still assumed Archer meant to use both since he was stashing our suitcase below and not on top of this one.

After a minute, he closed the laptop and I heard the bed scrunch as he stood. "Where do you want this?"

"Here with my stuff. What'd you think?" I caught the laptop from him and settled it with my other gear.

"You know it's 'iron hold,' right?"

"What?"

"You said, 'steel hold.' That's not a thing. It tripped me up. It's 'iron hold.'"

"Metal's metal."

"No...it's kind of not."

Warm cotton fell on my head. Archer standing beside me, between the two beds and pulling his shirt off.

I folded this in my lap as well.

"And you want 'concrete', not 'cement.' A lot of people use cement when they mean concrete."

"What's the difference?"

"Cement is one of the ingredients used to make concrete. The sidewalk itself is concrete."

"I didn't realize that." I weaseled out of my jeans, not wanting to stand all the way up and then have to hop on one foot to get them loose. I'd always had terrible balance with my eyes closed. "So that's what you thought? That I mixed my materials?"

"It did jump out." Archer opened the button and fly of his jeans. "These things would be a treat for a bacteriologist. Two days of plane and city? Ultimate bus pants."

I reached to catch the alleged hazardous material but found no one there. Archer had deliberately sidestepped me, chuckling. I have no idea where this sadistic streak comes from. He's the caretaker type most of the time, the tough love type maybe a quarter, and occasionally...just a total ass.

"I folded your shirt," I said. "You don't have to be a jerk."

"It's going into the laundry anyway," Archer said, still cheerful.

"And this is the first honeymoon night rerun. What's going to happen to this marriage if you can't be civil on the first night?"

"I'm sorry. Did I hurt your feelings?"

I moved fast this time, caught him around the waist, and threw him back against the first bed. The metal frame clanged on the wall. Archer was laughing at me. He grabbed my hair, dragged my face against his to kiss me, and I knew I would have to keep badgering him to get any real feedback about the second scene of my story.

But not right then. At the moment, I was on top of him, tongue in his mouth, feeling over his chest and down. On my honeymoon. I didn't mind waiting a few minutes for feedback. Or an hour or so. Or all night.

Chapter Ten

BRRRRING! WHOOSH!

Thundering feet, chattering crowds, push and shove of motion. We moved block by block, Archer stopping often to catch his breath as he tried to explain the sights to me.

"Brick bridge with three arches over this canal intersection. It's beautiful. Hundreds of years old. I don't know how some of the canal boats can go under it, though, the arches are so narrow. There are boats tied all the way down this one, and houseboats. It looks like all houseboats on the other side."

"Like the bikes?" I asked.

"Yeah, not so many chained bikes over here. I guess they're all out in rush hour."

It was Monday morning. After a Sunday spent mostly near "home," pulling ourselves together and still being jet-lagged, we had set out early to explore more of the city on foot and by those light rail trams or whatever they were that took us from the central station to the middle of the street drop-off.

I told him I wanted him to take me to the Red Light District—just so he had to tell me what he saw. And Archer wanted to see old churches and the street markets and all the canals and the tulip market.

No one had warned us that rush hour in Amsterdam was like stepping onto I-5 on a Monday morning, in which every car was transformed into four bicycles. And the whole interstate was two feet wide.

At least, this was how Archer summed it up after the fifth or sixth time he almost knocked me down or yanked me off my feet getting us both out of the way.

And, to think, we had wanted to get married and travel in October especially for it being the quiet time of year. After school was in. Before the holidays. Cheaper prices. Still good weather.

Archer led us up long sidewalks toward what he said was the center of town, following his map to a fry place that they had told us at the hostel were the best in Amsterdam. Even when we hit moments of relative peace without all the noise and people brushing past, Archer was endlessly moving left or right, stopping, indicating what was wrong.

"Pole—right to avoid a hole—jagged sidewalk—pole—curb down—curb up—pole—right to avoid a drop."

"What's up with the poles and holes?" I asked, straight-faced.

Archer, tense as a cop without coffee, did not find me amusing. "The sidewalks are damn narrow and there's... stuff everywhere. There are steps jutting out into them for doorways with a pole at the bottom starting handrails, leaving anyone walking on the sidewalk about a foot of space before stepping into the street. But there are also doorways down all along the way and those are just stairways, amounting to huge holes cut out of the sidewalk to go down to people's front doors. There's no rail or curb or anything. If you weren't watching or out in the dark or drunk, you would just step off into a hole five or six times on every sidewalk."

I almost had to give up the cane, keeping it scarcely inches in front of my feet, feeling the rough sidewalk and avoiding tripping. Archer had to react too fast, shift us too much—while also being mindful of bikes and cars flying past inches to our right and other humans crowding the sidewalks—for canes to be real help.

I felt bad for him. But we had already been through that. I refused to marry him for a long time exactly because of this kind of thing. It wasn't even that I was having a lousy time. I didn't mind the traveling. It was trashing the experience for the person I loved most that was bringing me down.

We did at last reach the fries and got an early lunch. Standing to eat in an alley: paper cones of amazingly crisp and hot potato strips in one hand, eating with the other, dipping into a glob of sauce on top—red pepper for Archer, pickle for me. Now, I like dill pickle, I'll eat any pickle—sweet, tart, spicy, seasoned. But this was the most blow-your-tongue-off vinegar dill of any dill pickle I'd ever tasted.

We got another fry cup with their house mayonnaise. Archer usually can't stand mayonnaise, but it cooled both our mouths.

While we ate, I tried to get more out of him about my story.

We had never progressed any farther in that regard on Saturday night. All through Sunday, it had come up a couple times, but Archer just wasn't very helpful. He'd told me to write more and stop worrying about what other people thought until I was really ready for feedback.

But I was ready. Obviously. Or I wouldn't keep asking.

If Archer was writing, he would get through five drafts before ever letting anyone see it. If then. Maybe never. It would never be perfect enough for him. I don't understand that. How are you going to get it perfect if you don't know what a reader thinks?

After dragging a little feedback from him on Sunday morning, I had managed to get in more writing time yesterday.

Archer had lain on his back. I was part on top of him, head on his chest, legs drawn up since the bed was not only narrow but too short. Our neighbors crashed around in the hall as if they were trying to move a piano in there. Someone pounded on a door and shouted for a long time before someone else finally answered. I also listened to Archer's heartbeat and traffic outside and dog tags jingle far down the street.

Archer had said I was info-dumping, instead of letting things move like a comic book, hitting people over the head with the fact that the lead was blind.

I said that was kind of the key point of the hero. People had to know.

"Is it? The key point is not that he's a superhero who can see into the future and past? The key point is not that he helps to solve crimes and obviously has a history with these villains? It's not the setting you're presenting? Which seems to be 'change one thing,' right? Modern urban where there happens to be a few super-powered people running around? You really feel like the key point of what you're writing is that the main character is blind?"

I'd had to think about that. I went on lying still, wishing the people down the hall were not so set on getting in the way of my hearing Archer living.

I trailed my fingertips from his jaw, down his neck, along his shoulder, across his arm, finally to his hand, then back up to his chest.

"What else?" I asked at last, still having to think about what he already said. I never usually found myself without a retort. That question of the key points had gotten to me.

"Is the dog's name for Daredevil? You're probably better off disassociating—"

"He was the first blind superhero—"

"And you're making something new. Not an imitation."

"It's a tribute," I said. Like Bowyer. But Archer hadn't mentioned that and I wasn't even sure if he'd made the connection.

"And isn't there another dog named Devil? One of the old serials? Was it *The Phantom*?"

Oh. Had to think about that one also.

"You spend too much time on kind of...stage direction, you know?" Archer went on.

"No."

"Every step of getting out of the car. Every turn of the dog. We don't need to know that stuff. Think about comic books and panels. Steps out. Walks on sidewalk, faces house, guy comes down from house. You're not going to have every line this guy is saying to his dog. And, frankly, people don't care. He's got a guide dog. Great. No one cares what it's trained to do. It's weird because you're not even like that. You're funny, Noah." He shifted in bed, trying to look at me, though I kept my head down against his chest. "Just a touch hyper, in case you hadn't noticed. Those are really good things for comic books. Don't get bogged down in stage direction.

"And how come there's not more tension with the police and this guy? They call in a private individual to figure stuff out for them, yet won't hire him on? If they don't like him, or there's some history, is this guy *trying* to help and being pushed back? Because that conflict right at the start would be more interesting. Like he shows up, but they don't want him, he's having to push just to be allowed to feel out the scene. I don't know...

"This is why you shouldn't let people read something that's two pages. You really need to let readers see your setup more and who everyone is before they can give feedback."

"What about the character?" I asked. "I wanted to make him have his own thing. There's nothing 'fixing' him from being blind. He's just blind. He has a dog and a stick. But he sees into the past and the future. That's what the superpower is. I don't think anyone's ever done that with a character like this before. It's not a rip-off."

"No." Archer had laughed a little. "It's so not. And it's brilliant. That part...that's really, really good."

That bit carried me through all of Sunday and last night with a new fluffiness in my soul. Like snuggling up inside that *stamppot* gravy boat. Then we stepped out into bicycle rush hour on Monday morning and all hell broke loose.

But I was still enjoying my stay. Besides worrying for Archer.

On our third paper cone of fries, I asked Archer if he would just humor me a little bit more with reading my next scenes, maybe some changes also, then I'd go in for a long stretch once we got home and wouldn't ask him again for a while.

"Yeah right." I could hear his smile.

His head was bowed beside mine, holding the fries for us, both leaning into a cold stone wall, close in the nippy autumn air.

"Sure," Archer continued. "If you're really wanting me to, I'll keep reading. You do need to work more, though, Noah."

"I know. I get that."

"Could have fooled me. You have mayonnaise on your nose."

"Lick it off," I said.

Archer chuckled.

"Will you ever get used to 'married' in public as well as private?" Exasperated, I wiped the back of my hand across my nose. "I'm not asking you to take your clothes off."

"I'm not going to lick your nose in public, Noah. I'm not your dog."

"Sometimes I wish you acted a bit more like one. You could learn a lot from Luath."

"Sorry she didn't bring you on this trip."

"You know what I mean," I said. "Just relax a little. You can kiss me in public and no one's going to lynch you. Not in Seattle and not in Amsterdam. If you start wanting to travel places where they would...you should maybe go on your own."

"I'm sorry I'm not as loving as your dog—"

"You know that's not what I mean also," I said. "It's not about love. It's about comfort in expression, in your own skin, in your own freedom to be yourself. I just thought you'd feel better about touching in public once we were married. I know this was a big step for you with your family. Sorry. I didn't mean to argue about it." *But if you were a straight newlywed and I was a woman, you'd have licked the mayonnaise off my nose and laughed and not thought anything of it.*

Would he, though...? I might have been underestimating the aloof thing.

Archer said nothing. The paper cone was nearly empty.

"Can we get more fries?" I asked.

"For real?"

"I'm hungry." I bit my lip. "You said this was the cheapest food you'd seen here."

"It's probably not good for you to eat three pounds of fried potatoes in one sitting, Noah."

"I'm on vacation. And I want to try the mustard sauce."

"There's a line now. Want to come over and wait with me or just stay here?"

"To be with you."

We waited in line together, Archer reading me all the sauce options. Ahead of us, it sounded like almost everyone got mayonnaise of some sort. The thing to do.

After a final fry cone—Archer only ate a few and I was actually feeling delightfully full for the first time since the Japanese noodles—we started off walking once more.

More crowds. We visited a few shops smelling of antiques and the kind of ancient paper that is not exactly moldy, but you know at a sniff you're surrounded by historic reading material. Despite being a computer programmer, Archer is into things like that.

Then the tulip market, smelling entirely different, and another grocery store for a couple snack foods—no peanut butter—so we weren't spending so much on food out. Every meal in this city was about fifty dollars for portions that left both of us hungry on our way out the door. And we never ordered drinks besides water—which we were also charged for.

Back at the hostel in the afternoon, while Archer left for the bathroom, I opened one of the coconut, date, and nut bars he'd gotten for us, thinking about those pricey dinners.

I wouldn't have thought anything of the door or wall banging, already used to noise around here, but it started while I was halfway through my bar, still going on when I finished. And the place had been quiet when we got back.

I left my wrapper on the table, assuming there was a wastebasket in the room, but unsure where it was, and went to the door to listen, opening it a crack, cane in my hand.

"Noah!" Down the hall.

It was Archer pounding on a door somewhere and calling for me.

Chapter Eleven

I MADE SURE my room key was in my pocket, felt the number on the door to remind myself of it before leaving, and set out with the cane down the hall to my left. Banging growing louder as I neared. Fourteen steps and the cane hit a wall. I made sure it was a wall, not a door. Noise now just to my right. Open air there, the hall making an L-turn. I followed this another six steps and heard the banging right in front of me. Door at the end of the hall, which the cane struck.

"Archer?"

"Noah? Christ, I thought you'd never come down here."

"What are you doing in someone else's room? I know Amsterdam has a reputation, but I don't recall discussing this marriage being open—"

"Noah, go downstairs and get someone at the front desk. The damn door locked. The other bathroom was being cleaned, so I came down here. It's just a unisex toilet and sink in this one. Obviously, the cleaner left immediately after because I've been hammering for minutes. I can't get the door open. Go down and—"

"This must be what all the banging was about on Sunday morning." I felt down the side of the door, found the knob, turned, and pushed it open.

Archer stopped abruptly.

"How'd you do that?" Now his voice was directly before my face, not coming through the heavy door.

"I turned the knob and opened the door. The inside knob must just get jammed."

"Why don't they fix it?"

"Maybe it's like an inside joke? These people eat chocolate and white bread and rancid nuts for breakfast."

Archer let out a breath. "Thanks."

"Let's use the one to the right from now on." I started back to the turn in the hall.

"It's a good thing you were here. I could have been stuck in there for hours on a Monday afternoon with no one in."

"Yeah, well—" I made the turn back to the left. Fourteen steps. "I wasn't going anywhere. Those coconut bars you got are good. Do you want one?"

"Sure. Since we know we're not getting much for dinner."

"How about pizza? We could get a big pizza. That's got to be cheaper than what we've been trying." I felt our room number.

"Good idea." He let out another breath, waiting while I opened the door. "I'll look it up."

"And I'll go ask downstairs. I need to practice getting back and forth anyway—in case of emergencies." I was grinning, though Archer's tone was not amused. Archer and his claustrophobia and his perfectionism would not have handled being blind very well. Then again, I was a comic book, art, and video game addict in my teens. I wouldn't have said I'd manage well blind either.

"Sure. You ask," he said. "I'll research. Then...let's go for a walk in the park across the street before we go to dinner. It's starting to rain again, so maybe we can have a moment of peace out there. It looks like a really nice park. Like Golden Gate or Central Park."

"Craving some wide-open spaces?" Still grinning.

"It's not funny, Noah. And you've got a lot of nerve throwing stones since you completely freak out when you're upset about your own spatial dilemmas."

"That's different. I'm helpless."

"Bullshit. Go ask. And tell them about that damn door."

I left, smirking.

We did find a pizza place by recommendation and first went for a walk in Vondelpark in a slight drizzle, temperature dropping.

Archer was right. I heard a few steps, a few jingling dogs, a bike or two, but the park was remarkably quiet and open in the rain on a chilly Monday afternoon.

We talked about getting the bag back, how much we were used to taking clothes for granted, what kind of pizza we wanted—we both would eat anything—and about the noise in the hostel.

"It's gorgeous," Archer said about the park, holding my hand like we were normal people. It was the first time we had stepped outside in Amsterdam together and he was not tense as a cat on a wire. "Absolutely huge. I forget we're in a city at all. It's all green carpets and ponds, sculptures here and there, walking paths. The trees are part green and part yellow and red and pink, mostly just starting to turn, but some have leaves down already. It's beautiful."

"Maybe we should start all our days here instead of in bicycle hell?"

"I'm really sorry about the bikes, Noah—"

"What? Like you put them there?" I laughed at him.

Again, Archer did not sound amused. "I know. I'm just sorry about shoving you around so much. And those stupid sidewalks. I had no idea how safety-obsessed the States are. There's a broken neck and a lawsuit every three steps here. I guess the Dutch just don't think like that."

"Doesn't mean we're the ones who are right. *Obsessed* is not a healthy way to be either."

"I know, we're supposed to be here to see the culture and all that. Not impress ours. That's not the point of travel. It's just a little hard to accept feeling like a whole society, at least one particular metropolitan city, has contempt for any human being who is not totally physically and mentally fit and capable. I mean, I wouldn't want to walk around Amsterdam if I had a crutch or if I was over sixty years old, or under sixteen, or hard of hearing, or had the sun in my eyes. Really, it's like an Olympic sport just going from one address to another."

"And this is *off*-season," I said.

"God, don't say that. I can't imagine." He sighed.

"Sorry, Archer. I guess you were right. I shouldn't have pushed you to come here when you said we should start out with smaller trips. I just thought...this was the goal, right? So why not?"

Archer had been all for a quiet honeymoon to Victoria at first, maybe San Francisco. I was the one who'd told him if this was the city at the very top of his list, and now we had the chance, we should go. With the gift tickets and the hostel, it really didn't cost much more than spending a week away locally.

Now, I wished for once in my life that I'd kept my mouth shut. Archer knew this was too much to start out. Our first big trip. A trip that should have been a celebration for the two of us. We should have gone ahead with a summer wedding and driven to Ocean Shores.

"It's not your fault either," Archer said. "You were right. I really, really wanted to come. It's breathtaking. I'm not sorry we're here. I just didn't think through it enough."

I smiled. "You're sure that's the problem? Only you overlooking all those chapters in the travel guides headed, *What You Need to Know About Amsterdam Before Traveling with the Visually Disabled*, right?"

Archer laughed. "Yeah...I guess, there wasn't a lot of early warning. There's a pond, almost a lake, up here and a mammoth water fountain."

"I hear it. Take a picture for Shiloh."

"I got a few of the canals for her." Archer, who never was a photographer, stopped to fish in his coat pocket for his phone.

Shiloh had a thing about water lately. She was an artist like the rest of us, besides my dad, but she went more and more into photography and was really going all out with it now, working and going to school from home. Water was a big deal all of a sudden. She spent so much time trying to tell me about how this or that reflection or spray or light through water looked in her pictures, I wished I could see just so she would shut up.

Archer snapped pictures as we walked around the pond and started down a wet gravel and dirt path.

I could not hear a single voice or step or wheel anymore.

"I'm glad you're not sorry we came here," I told him. "Because I'm not. I'm sorry you're having a tough time. And I'm sorry about the bag and the storm and the bathroom door and the price of food. I'm sorry you're stressed out. But not that we came here. It could have been a long time before we had another chance like this."

"I know. That's why I'm also glad we came."

He spoke next to my ear, hand pressure marginally tighter on my own left hand as he leaned in toward my left side. I turned my head and he kissed me while we walked. Then I knew for sure we were alone. Maybe he was also remembering the earlier conversation over the fries and just wanted to prove to me that he would touch me in public—yet he wasn't fooling me about our current isolation.

The only time Archer had ever kissed me with a bunch of people around, *ever*, was on our wedding day. And then only because he was told to. I'd wondered even then if he would, but he got through it.

One step at a time. Years ago, when I ruthlessly pursued him in high school and he squirmed half out of his skin just being around me, he would never have even held my hand in public.

When you look for silver linings, for what came out of a total shit situation that was slightly less shitty, Archer learning to let me touch him due to my loss of sight had to be one of the best for me. It changed me as a person. It brought me a love of literature and introduced Luath into my life. But Archer's hand in mine, him kissing me in the rain in a park in a foreign city in the middle of almost a million people—even if out of range—that was the best.

We turned. Raindrops clattered on leaves just over our heads. Archer told me we were walking between thick trees, heading for an arching footbridge.

The perfect place to push my luck and try to get into his pants?

Archer said to wait a moment as we stepped to the middle of the sloping bridge so he could take another picture, then moved again to kiss me, which I returned, holding his lips with mine, touching his face, feeling the back of his neck wet with cold rain.

I found I could not do it—not push him. It just wouldn't have been worth breaking the spell. Here; hands and faces. Back in the room; pants. Where I knew Archer would have no objections to my removing them for him.

Scene Three

DR. CHAMAELEO SITS in his office of materials: leather and silk, paper and steel, granite and dried flowers, soap and oil. Every color, every texture, every sight and touch can be experienced on a tiny scale in that office. His desk is comprised of several different woods and metals with a top that is part glass, part copper, part maple. His chair is chrome and vinyl.

Dr. Chamaeleo cannot be seen as an individual person sitting at his desk on his chair. He is only a vague shape among endless detail.

His hand on the desk, moving over a keyboard, looks exactly like the keyboard, yet flickers of shadow separate the two, flesh from plastic.

The screen glows in the dim room like a TV on after dark.

Dear Whiteout,
My compliments to the chef. We must arrange a tasting sometime. I can hardly wait.

He signs off, pausing a moment and drumming his fingers before adding:

Yours truly,
Dr. Chamaeleo

He has stood up from the desk when he notices a new message in the inbox. An answer so fast seems hardly possible, but he sits back down to open it.

How did you know it was me?

Dr. Chamaeleo frowns over this. Wasn't it obviously his work? The small house, the bodies, the numbers. Yet ... there had been something odd about them. Women this time? Was Whiteout trying to cover his trail all of a sudden?

More finger drumming.

Wasn't it?

Another instant answer: *Did they call in the blind one?*

Dr. Chamaeleo wrote back: *Not while I was there. Only police.*

A few more seconds, then: *Tasting party, tomorrow night. Meet Lucas at Volunteer Park. North end. 9:00 p.m.*

Chapter Twelve

I WOKE UP late, remembering the night before. After pizza, Archer had showered while I'd jotted down a quick scene. I'd kept him company to update family and friends back home by email, though he did the writing, then we'd put the electronics away to undress each other.

I had blindfolded him, having brought the silk blindfold with me. It got Archer to play fair. Still, I had to keep tabs on him or he would sneak it off and not tell me. He's not very obedient.

We stayed up late, starting to feel in tune with the time zone, remembering to enjoy our honeymoon. And I had the idea before falling asleep, curled against Archer, thinking of the park and pizza and his body and him having sneaked off his blindfold after all. By the time I reached to take it off, it was gone.

"I kept my eyes closed," Archer said, laughing while I punched his shoulder and asked him if no one had ever told him as a kid not to be a cheater.

Then, in those minutes before sleep when you know for a moment you are falling asleep, I'd known what we needed for tomorrow. I even started to stir myself, to tell him, share my own brilliance. Yet Archer was also falling asleep, his heartbeat and breath slow and regular in my ear, his muscles finally relaxed.

Now I woke with the idea following my mind, running back in a moment as I remembered that there had been something I wasn't supposed to forget.

"Archer?"

"Hmm?" Awake, he shifted and ran a hand through my hair. Medium brown hair last time I'd looked. Though that was a good many years ago. For all I knew, Archer had me getting a shampoo that was slowly turning it green.

These are the kinds of things that cross your mind when you're blind and newly married to a very wonderful man who occasionally has a strangely twisted sense of humor.

I turned my face up to kiss his palm, regretting moving at once and pressing my face back into his skin.

"Why is it so cold in here? It feels like January."

"You know I can't sleep with the window closed. And it's not that cold. It's only cracked an inch."

"Let's double up the covers."

"We did. After the last time you complained." Archer leaned up a few inches, reaching to grab an edge of the second duvet and pull it up to my ears and his shoulder. "Could put something on to sleep in, also. What if there's a fire alarm?"

"I've got nothing to hide."

"I actually wasn't thinking about you being embarrassed, Noah. I know that doesn't happen easily. I was thinking about you being cold and standing on the street at night during a fire alarm naked."

"What are the odds?"

"The way this trip has been going?"

"Good point. I'll make sure I have everything hanging on the foot of the bed for me to reach next time. You're distracting me. I had something important to say."

"Uh-huh."

"I can't remember. What are you doing?"

"Reading about Amsterdam museums on my phone." He shifted again, turning more onto his back. "You know, we're over half done with the trip. I can't believe how fast it's gone and we haven't really gotten to much."

"That's just what I wanted to talk to you about," I said. "I remember."

"Go for it."

"You've got to get out and see some of that stuff. What you care the most about. You should spend today out on your own—"

"Yeah, no, Noah. That's kind of not the honeymoon point."

"But going to Amsterdam to stay in a hostel is? Come on, Archer. We knew this was unconventional. It's not about 'traditional' honeymoons, is it? If we were all into tradition, we could have started by marrying women, for one thing.

"I had about five minutes to sit down and think about my comic book yesterday. I'll get breakfast with you, then you go to the top museums you want to see. I'll stay here all day and try to get some stuff done that I also care about. We have plenty of snacks here now. I'll go downstairs if I need anything. They would even help me get takeout. Everyone at the front desk has been really nice and I'm a sympathetic character—"

Archer snorted.

"I know you don't want to feel like you're just going to leave me behind for a good time on your own. I get that. I'm not trying to ditch you, either. But I'm really, really okay with you out alone. I'm also perfectly comfortable going downstairs to talk to people if I want to. Everyone speaks English. Especially the young people around here."

I finally ran out of words, Archer saying nothing while I caught my breath.

"I thought about it last night," I said. "Don't be silly and miss your most important to-do stuff here just because it would be crazy hard to go there with me. We're not likely to come back to Amsterdam anytime soon."

Archer let out a breath.

I kissed his neck.

He did not push me away or even comment.

"Okay," he said after a moment.

"It's all right to go off and do something fun, Archer." I kissed my way to his jaw. "You don't have to be upset about it."

"I just don't want to leave you sitting in a room all day."

"I'm not a puppy. And I'm not you. I'll go downstairs and hang out with people. I'll be happy to do that. There are always people down there in the afternoon and evening. Then you and I will get dinner together whenever you get back. No rush, maybe that Japanese noodle place again that's open late, and you can tell me where you went."

"Okay…" He kissed me, lips closed, gentle. "Love you."

"Before your parting words, I do want you to take me down to breakfast."

"Deal. I need to get going." He kissed me again, then pushed me away and I sat up so he could climb from bed.

Chapter Thirteen

OF COURSE, MY writing binge did not last.

I started, I stopped, I tried to chat with Shiloh, I started again, wrote a bit of a scene that didn't make sense, sent some emails. Twiddled my thumbs. Huh.

Maybe Archer was right about my inability to live a happy, internalized life for a few hours. Then again, there was no reason I shouldn't go hang out with people downstairs. None at all. That's what travel was about, in a way.

Archer wouldn't come back and say, "How many pages did you write?" He would just ask if everything was okay.

I wanted to be able to tell him I had a good time more than that I wrote ten new scenes.

Thinking of Archer asking about my well-being got me thinking about him and last night and being married to him. It didn't matter that we had been living together—now and then—for a few years. If anything, it made this new adventure better. We didn't have to work out the awkward bits.

But now there was more. A new chapter to explore. And it should have been all good. All moving forward. What we had before was good. What we would have now would get better and better. This was more than just about legal paperwork. It was a commitment, a promise, a lifestyle.

A lifestyle that I had tried to keep Archer from being bound to in the first place. One his family was not exactly thrilled by. One our families thought we were awfully young for. Archer had been a bit of an old man ever since I'd known him. I wasn't worried about our ages. How many years did you have to be in love before other people believed you knew it? And that you were in love enough to stay that way? And why should we have to prove anything to other people in the first place?

Then it turned out Archer was just that inch more stubborn than myself to wait me out and I'd said yes and here we were. Better and better. Right?

So why was I sitting alone in a hostel room thinking about what was off-kilter instead of cheerfully writing my next scene as I had planned?

What part of this wasn't better?

Not that Archer wasn't with me. I was glad of that. He could see what he wanted to. I could do some work. We didn't have to be with each other every second. He needed space. He'd always been one who needed space.

Then what was it?

I drummed my fingers on the tabletop and blew out my cheeks, wanting to get up and pace.

What?

Archer left. Good.

Yet Archer had not volunteered to leave. He had come to his senses about running back to the airport alone, and that ended up being great. No problem for me, an easy job for him. This time, I'd had to say something, had to push him away. And I shouldn't have. Because it meant he wasn't willing to say for himself that he needed a day out on his own to properly experience this place, to have a few hours in his own fairy-tale city and just take it in.

It wasn't his leaving. I truly, honestly, at the bottom of my soul, wanted him out on his own for a while. No, what was nagging me was that he hadn't said he needed that time out. I'd had to think of it. Which meant he wasn't looking after himself. Only me. Which was the whole goddamned reason in the first place I'd told him I didn't want to be his husband. Because I was scared I would destroy his life by claiming it. And that, yes, in that regard we were both way too young. Archer had fifty or sixty or seventy years of life ahead of him to live. And at twenty-four, I'd let him clamp on an ultimate ball and chain and throw away the key.

What I still could not sort out in my own mind was whether I was more upset with myself for allowing this to happen or at Archer for not just saying this morning, or last night, or three days ago, *I need a day or two out on my own in this city. How can we make that work for both of us so you're comfortable?*

So simple. But he wouldn't. Because that was his dominant caretaker trait.

I'd just have to do it for him. For the rest of our lives? *Don't worry about that right now.*

Right now, just this trip. We had a few days left. At least I could see what was going on. At least I could do a few small things of my own to take care of him.

So, I did not actually get much done. But I did think. Which, as Shiloh had often been eager to tell me, was not a given in my case.

Speaking of which, since the chatting had failed, I had a new email from my sister. I frowned as I listened to it. She had taken Luath to the dog park and Luath played endlessly with a young beagle. Best of pals now, apparently. A beagle seemed rather degrading to Luath's standards—being the most beautiful and intelligent golden retriever on the planet—but maybe my selfless dog was doing the little hound a favor.

I sent a note back, thanking Shiloh for getting her out.

Obviously not writing, so I pushed back the chair and grabbed the cane.

Wishing I had Luath with me—unlike Archer, Luath was God's gift to breaking the ice—I went downstairs at 2:00 p.m.

The evening shift must have just changed downstairs because I was greeted by the same voice who met us on our first night in.

I told her I stayed in that day to work.

She asked if she could do anything for me. A bad start. You have to get these people past the pity tone and then they'll loosen up and make themselves useful. From her, useful meant introductions to anyone hanging out in the party room. A room that probably had a technical name—lounge or something—but I knew it only from grabbing snack foods at breakfast and the blasting music and noise we walked past in the evenings.

Now, I already heard music. A good sign.

"I just wanted to see who was around," I told her, smiling. "Sounds like someone. I'm Noah, by the way."

"I'm Anna." Looking at me when she spoke, which was nice. Also a smile now. I could usually hear a smile, with better accuracy even than I could feel color. "If you have time, I'll introduce you to my cousin and her friend. They're visiting from the south and they wanted to meet this crowd too. They're about your age, I'd say."

"I'd love to. Are they here now?"

"I just had a text from Elly. She's on her way if you want to hang out. Can I...show you around?" With a bit of an uncertain laugh.

"That'd be great. Archer just rushes through everywhere and I'm not even sure how to get around the room." Gesturing vaguely toward the music.

Anna was excellent. She walked around the space with me, didn't mind me taking her elbow when I explained that was the simplest system for me, cane in my right hand. I laughed at them playing American pop music and she said most of the TV and movies and music she had grown up with was British and American, which I found disheartening. It takes so much wonder out of travel if we're all going to listen to Justin Bieber.

We were back in the lobby when she had to answer questions from a couple of men who addressed Anna in German. She chatted away with them, me not understanding a word. So that made fluent Dutch, English, and German. What else? Probably French, at least. Travel was also making me feel really stupid. You'd think I'd know a bit more after all the reading I did.

Soon enough, cousin Elly and friend showed up and I had more to entertain me.

Elly and Marike were, in fact, the highlights of my day. They were university students spending a week off in the city with Elly's aunt and cousin, Anna. I was not clear on whether they were officially out of school this week, some kind of autumn break, or if they only came here on a whim, playing hooky. I didn't ask.

Elly's English was so flawless, I could hardly even hear her accent, though Marike, also an English speaker, had a noticeable accent and hesitated on the rare word. They laughed when I commented on their speech, confirming what Anna told me about American and British TV and movies.

"Ever read American comic books?" I asked as we sat around on an old sofa and chairs in the lounge. "I'm working on one."

"How?" Elly still sounded close to laughing.

I was delighted by the question. Americans can be too politically correct around blind people. If I told a stranger at home I was working on a watercolor painting, they'd probably say how nice that sounded—and no more.

I told them I was still trying to figure out how to be my own artist, but could at least write the outline with my tactile and audio interface on my laptop. They were intrigued, a far better audience than most Americans as well.

Then I had to ask about them—what did they look like and why were they in Amsterdam and what were they going to school for.

"I have never had to tell anyone how I look," Marike said with a nervous, embarrassed laugh. "Where do you start?"

"Tell me about each other," I suggested.

"Here is Marike," Elly said smoothly. Her voice was chipper and light and had a little cheerleader behind it. I loved it. "She wears blue jeans and long coats and boots, making her look even taller than she is."

"Is she tall?" I asked, though I could tell by the locations of their voices before we'd all sat down that both young women were tall.

"As tall as you," Elly said. "I'm not so tall—"

"Don't say anything about yourself," I said.

"Oh, yes." Elly giggled. "She has dark brown hair, brunette, and big hazel eyes and a very big nose ring."

Both girls burst out laughing.

"No nose ring?" I asked.

"No nose ring," Marike repeated firmly. "But Elly has rings in her eyebrows."

"Are you just saying that?"

"Just one," Elly said. "And my ears."

"What else about Elly?"

"She's blonde and she is...hasty?"

"Impulsive?" I asked.

"That's it," Marike said. "She is very impulsive. She owns two hundred hats and wears a different hat for each day of the week. Pink hats, red hats, rain hats, winter hats, sun hats, she wears hats like some women wear shoes."

"Cute hats?" I asked.

Both laughing again.

"I wouldn't wear them if they weren't cute," Elly said.

"You brought all those hats with you to Amsterdam? Is that all that's in your bag?"

"One bag for clothes. One bag for hats," Elly said, still giggling. "Here, this is my hat today."

I reached up as she shifted in her chair in front of me. She pressed a somewhat stiff felt hat into my hands. I felt the small brim all the way around for rain or sun, the warmth of it from being on her head, smelled the scent of perfumed shampoo and just a hint of cat.

I passed it back. "I also like red."

They did not laugh. There was a pause.

"How did you know it was red?" Marike asked.

"I'm good with colors. You said she had red hats and it felt red."

Another pause.

"How does something feel red?" Elly sounded genuinely fascinated. I heard her replacing her hat on her head not far from my own face.

I shrugged. "I don't know. How does something look red? How does a hamburger smell like a hamburger? You know what else I noticed about your hat?"

"What's that?"

I could feel the interest dripping off them like balm, both leaning in toward me as if they thought I would start doing magic tricks. I should have been coming down here every day.

"It was bone dry. I didn't know it was nice out today. It's rained almost since we got here. A fine day for it to be nice when I'm staying in."

"Come out with us," Elly squealed. "Why are you here all alone?"

"I'm supposed to be working on my comic book, but I'm procrastinating."

"Procrastinate with us. We're going shopping."

"For hats?"

Both laughed—more.

"But, really, you don't want to take me shopping. I'm a lot of responsibility on busy streets. I walk into things."

"We won't let you crash if you want to come out with us," Marike said. "Uptown Vondelpark Hostel is right next door to the most...high..."

"High-end? Posh?"

"Yes, posh shopping in Amsterdam."

"Tell you what: if you'll show me around the neighborhood, I'll get us all something to eat. I was hoping to try all the fries in the city."

Couldn't afford to start promising extra meals in this place, but maybe I could get away with snacks for three with my own confidence in different sized bills.

They told me they would be happy to "show" me around and I didn't owe them anything.

I was amazed, when we stepped out, to discover sunlight blazing down on us. The air was cool and bright, the sun wonderful after all the cold rain on my face lately.

The two young women told me about their schoolwork. Marike wanted to be a veterinarian and Elly was studying fashion and design.

Archer and I had figured out our own system over time. My mom and Shiloh had been around from the start as well.

So I had never actually needed to explain to anyone how to help me get around for more than some tiny thing, like Anna inside.

With dark glasses on and my cane, I told them I needed to hold an arm or shoulder, not them hold onto me, that not steering me into pits or posts or other people would be nice, and that a few notes about the scenery also enlivened my experience.

The two were great. Not embarrassed or shy about me touching them, eager to tell me about the city and show off their own knowledge as non-natives themselves.

This was going to be fun.

Chapter Fourteen

"SO, HOW DID it go?" I asked Archer over dinner of hot noodles, which I had to eat ever so carefully. "Did you have fun?"

It had been late when he returned and we'd hurried to the restaurant without much of a moment to catch up.

"It went great. Amsterdam is just crazy. Crazy gorgeous, crazy weird. I went through three museums and two markets. I want to take you back to the bizarre, junky flea-market one. Your mom and sister would love it. We've got to take them something for looking after Luath."

"Chocolate will suffice for my mom. Didn't you say it's everywhere? But Shiloh would go for something bizarre at a Dutch flea market."

"Chocolate for both moms then. Your mom likes dark also, right? What about you? Did you get some scenes written?"

Hmm. And I'd thought he wouldn't ask.

"Sort of," I said.

"Does that mean no?"

"I'm thinking about it. These things take time."

"Uh-huh. What did you do?"

"I flirted with a couple of Dutch college students all afternoon."

Archer sighed. "I swear, Noah, you could turn a prison into a cookout in an afternoon."

"I don't know why you act like making friends is a bad thing."

"I'd ask if you made a cute threesome, but I'm going to assume you don't know."

"They sounded cute. I'm sure you'll see them yourself tomorrow. The girl who helped us the first night is the cousin of one. The cousin and the friend are staying in the city with them for a school break. They're coming through the hostel to hang out with people their own ages."

"So is this a couple?"

I opened my mouth, paused. "It hadn't occurred to me. No. They were too flirty, too fag-haggy."

"*Haggy* is not a—"

"Unless Dutch lesbians are just like that—"

"But both women?"

"Of course they're women. Guys make terrible tour guides—no offense. Not you. But you know what I mean. Guys want to see bars and sporting or military landmarks. We went shopping."

"Oh, God. Please don't tell me you spent all your cash."

"I only bought us pancakes. Awesome pancakes that you have to try. Nothing like American pancakes. But that was it. They were getting their own shoes. If we happen to cross paths tomorrow, we've got to get the address of the pancake place to go back. I don't think I'd be able to retrace our steps." I grinned into my noodle bowl.

Kind of weird that this day, the one away from Archer, had been my best in the city so far. But it wasn't just me. So much of this joy and new lightness in my chest came from knowing he'd been out and had a good time also.

A filling, delicious meal in a warm restaurant surrounded by other buzzing tourists was the cherry on top.

"So they got you around okay?" Archer asked. "It's a madhouse out there."

"They were like old pros," I said airily.

"I'm glad you had fun. Sorry you didn't get more writing work done."

"It's percolating. I told you. And they had ideas."

"Yeah?"

"Elly and Marike—rhymes with *eureka*, that's how you can remember."

"Got it." Archer was laughing a little.

"Both thought the comic was a brilliant idea. I don't know why you don't make friends when you're somewhere new."

"Because it would involve speaking to strangers?"

"Only for the first few minutes. Then they're not strangers." Now he really did laugh.

"Tell me about your museums," I said. "What'd you see?"

Archer took me back to the hostel after dinner, air bitter cold, telling me about the clear, starry sky and our breaths steaming before our faces in streetlamps. But dry and fresh out. I turned my head, finding his face, kissing his jaw as we walked in the cold.

Archer didn't exactly push me away, but he didn't return the kiss on the street either.

"Do your flirting Dutch friends know you're here on your honeymoon?"

"Of course they do. They wanted to meet you. I told them you were stunningly handsome and brilliant—"

"Really, Noah? Did they ask how you know?"

"Actually, they did. Elly was laughing at me saying what you looked like. Do you know, I worry sometimes that I'm forgetting? I remember you the most because I feel you. I don't have my hands on Shiloh's or Mom's faces all the time. I'm afraid I'll forget the faces of everyone I ever knew. It's well underway already. What if I forget your eyes? You have beautiful eyes."

"You're not going to forget my eyes."

"How do you know? I could forget the color blue."

"Here we are. Left into stairs going up. You definitely won't forget blue. You're too good with colors. And you had an advantage before all this."

We paused on the landing as Archer opened the door and I felt the frame with my cane.

"How's that?" I asked.

"You were an artist. You *are* an artist, even if you don't draw anymore. You have that sight in your mind. In your memory. You saw things, noticed things, took in things that other people never do, even when they have all their lives to look around them. That's a gift."

Archer led me through the noisy lobby, metal music booming now, many voices yammering in many languages. He opened the next door with his key and we started slowly up the two flights of stairs, echoing with our steps as the noise faded behind.

"You're not going to forget the color blue," Archer repeated. "You're not going to forget my face that you drew a million times. It's almost like...you were ready for this. That probably just sounds irritating to you. But so many people never really see, Noah. You did. Sometimes, I think...you still do."

"I love you," I said.

Archer laughed at me.

"Did you go to the torture museum?" I asked.

"It wasn't at the top of my list. Want to go tomorrow?"

"I don't like to make plans too far in advance."

"Speaking of plans... Shower? It's totally quiet up here."

He still would not join me, but Archer had helped me feel more comfortable in the hall bathroom, and having a moment when he would at least be in the shower room with me did make things more manageable.

We grabbed our gear and traded walking shoes for flip-flops in our room, then had quick, only mildly stressful showers before bed. With towels and the shower shoes, we didn't bother trying to get dressed or otherwise sort ourselves out in the bathrooms now. We just wrapped towels around our waists and hurried back to the room.

I hung onto Archer's arm as he yanked me along, then *wham*—my naked shoulder collided with the doorframe.

This sparked a round of swearing on my part, a lecture to be more careful on Archer's part, and me trying to push him into something solid and see how he liked it. He was amused by me, pulling my towel off.

"One day without me and you think you can forget your guiding manners." I caught the towel, yanking it back from him.

"You're so controlling," Archer said. "It's good for you every now and then. But I didn't mean for you to hurt yourself."

"Fun, though, wasn't it? Getting out, I mean—not abusing me. I wasn't the only one who had a good time. You had to have gotten a lot done."

"Sure I did."

"Red Light District?"

"I wasn't in that part of the city. But we'll go tomorrow if you want to double date. I'll pick up one of the ladies in the windows and you bring your new girlfriends."

"You did miss me after all," I said. "I knew you did."

Archer blew on the back of my neck, making me jump since he had been speaking right in front of me while I dried my hair. I don't know how he can move that stealthily. I threw an elbow and caught him in the chest. Not hard. He wasn't close enough. Laughing again.

"I did really miss you chatting people up for me," Archer admitted.

"I knew you would."

He touched my waist, about to put his arm around me from behind, but I swung the towel into his head with both hands, pillow-fight style.

Archer caught the towel and wrestled it from me. "That's okay. I don't really mind being on my own some. I know that's hard for you to comprehend."

Aha. I did know that. Knew he wouldn't admit to wanting time out alone. I didn't say it, though.

He kissed me, still struggling over rights to the towel. I pulled him around so he hit the bed first, myself following his motion.

Maybe we really should bring the girls out with us if they'd come. Then Archer and I could spend time together while he wasn't having to constantly look out for me.

"You're right," I said. "I just love being around people too much." I had his face in my hands, fingers in his wet hair, leaning in to kiss him as he sat up on the bed. "I have intimacy issues."

"What did you say?" Towel gone, Archer's hands stroked down from my shoulders to my hips.

I cut him off, my tongue between his teeth.

He grabbed my neck, pulling me down with him and breaking the kiss. "You have *boundary* issues, Noah," he went on. "*I* have intimacy issues." Another kiss, another break. "Where do you get this stuff?"

"I knew it was one or the other."

Archer laughed and I found his mouth again. I loved his voice and the feel of him, his sighs and the way I could hear him roll his eyes at me, and how he touched me. But, mostly, I loved his laugh. And how much I'd been hearing it this evening.

I tried to push his knees up. He tried to get me to sit on top of him.

"Such a control freak—" he started.

"*I'm* the control freak?"

"Stop—" Catching my hands.

"Like your overinterest in being top has nothing to do with control," I said.

"The bottom's always in control," Archer said, panting now and trying to shove me off. "Bottom controls everything. If he or she is not in control, it's called rape."

"I never thought of it that way. Although...seriously depressing when you say it like that."

"Sorry. But that's—*shit, Noah—*"

I chuckled and let go of his balls. "How much should superheroes in comic books have sex lives these days?"

"Is there still a censorship code?" He was sitting up again, pulling me down onto the bed instead, but gently now—with strokes and kisses instead of dragging me.

"I was thinking more independent anyway."

"Then you can do whatever you want, right?"

"I like doing whatever I want." I wrapped my arms around him, biting his neck.

"So I've noticed."

"Don't be complacent."

"I have no idea what word you meant this time." Archer sighed. "But that one was wrong."

"I'm glad you're here." I slithered onto my back, feeling down his body.

"Glad you said yes?" He followed me.

"Best decision I ever made."

"That, at least, sounds exactly right."

Chapter Fifteen

THE NEXT DAY, we ran into Elly and Marike downstairs on our way in from lunch at the park. Another sunny day and crowds everywhere, Archer tense again. We hadn't spent much time on the landscape or joy of the moment this time. More like playing Tetris—hurry and dodge and dart and turn, try to fit in just right and stay ahead of getting creamed.

I asked my friends about the pancake place when we met in the lobby. Then we discussed markets. Archer and I were soon heading back out to the junk market and they eagerly offered to join in.

I suspected Archer was taken aback by this. He thinks sociable people always have an ulterior motive because he does not understand that socializing can be the whole point.

They had been giggling and chatty with me. With both of us, they were even more involved, definitely falling for Archer—as everyone does. He has no idea how gorgeous and charismatic he is. Which is part of the effect, naturally.

It was a breath of fresh air, having them along. Marike helped me maneuver half the time, giving Archer a break to take pictures and chat with Elly about the city. She was swooning—I could hear it all over her high voice and light giggles.

I didn't mind. Never been the jealous type. I was just glad Archer put up with them—all three of us—laughing and giving him a hard time when I knew he would be much happier walking around on his own for a few hours.

The luster of flea markets loses something in darkness. Just like museums or any other sightseeing. Without all the junk to admire, there's just not much happening at a flea market besides a dangerous crowd. The three of them got on board talking about this one, though, and I haven't had such a good time shopping for old junk and handmade trinkets since I was ten and going to art shows with my mom.

When I could tell Archer was reaching his social limit, we exchanged email addresses and I told Elly and Marike to come by tomorrow night to hang out in the hostel.

Really, I wanted to ask them to come out with me again, let Archer go, but should talk to him about that first. Still, we were running out of time. I couldn't let Archer leave Amsterdam without checking all those boxes off his list.

Archer took me "home" when we split up, stopping for fries on the way. Then into a grocery store for a few more snacks. Archer said we had to get food ready for the flight back, three days away.

Him thinking about running out of time also.

Then the kicker:

"I'm sorry we haven't been spending more time together, Noah," Archer said as he walked to the hostel.

"You're crazy. We need to be *apart* more. What else do you have to get to in the city while you've still got a couple days?"

"I don't know. We've been all over. Here're the steps."

Upstairs, someone was banging on a door. Archer left me at our room to liberate the poor soul from the bathroom. He came back even tenser, muttering about the management of the hostel and why hadn't anyone done anything about it?

I wasn't paying attention, meeting him in the doorway. "I think you need to go out alone again tomorrow."

"That's not the point of a honeymoon," Archer snapped.

"It's not about the honeymoon. It's about this place. This is a big deal. You're letting it slip away."

"Spending time with you isn't letting anything slip away, Noah." He pushed past me in the tight space, pulling off his coat and not looking at me when he spoke.

"That's just sentimental," I said. "The whole reason we were going to give this a try was you assured me it wasn't going to destroy your own independence. We're in freaking Amsterdam. You can spend a couple days out. I don't know why you make such a big deal of everything."

"Give this a try?" He faced me. "That's what this is to you? Like a practice session?"

"That's not what I meant. You know it's not. Of course I'm not thinking of it like that." I remained standing against the shut door. "I'm just thinking that we knew there could be issues and it seems like this is one of them. You need some of your own time. You just reminded me that you *like* to be alone—"

"A generalization. On my honeymoon, I'd rather be with my new spouse—"

"And I don't mind you going out. At all—"

"What do you want?" Voice angry now, way past sighs. "You want me to dump you with your girlfriends and run around to see more sights on my own?"

"You are such a drama queen sometimes," I said. "I'm not a child. You're not 'dumping' anyone anywhere. But, yes, I think it would be a good idea for us to split up again. This is silly. The city's a death trap. If I do want to go out, they're more comfortable navigating here than you are."

"So you really would rather be out with them? You're taking the social thing a little too far. It's like a compulsion—"

"Now I'm the compulsive one also? Look in the mirror, Archer. Do you have something against Elly and Marike?"

"I have something against us each going off and doing our own thing the whole time—"

"Stop with the 'whole time' crap! You're talking about a couple days! You just don't like them. What is it? What's wrong?"

"I keep telling you what's wrong and you keep ignoring me!"

"Who's ignoring?" I asked. "You won't listen to a thing I say. You never have. I told you this was a bullshit idea in the first place, but you convened me about—"

"*Convinced*—"

"—the whole marriage thing and I *convinced* you about the trip and here we are. Now, instead of making the best of it, you're just going to shuffle around with me in a park and a few square blocks rather than doing what you care about."

"Spending time with you *is* what I care about!" Archer shouted.

"But we're in Amsterdam! We can sit at home together—since it's your favorite activity—in Seattle! Speaking of which, why don't we go downstairs to mingle with others like normal people do while traveling in an international hostel? Oh, no, you wouldn't want that. You might not like them. Because you never like any of my friends—"

"That's not even true—"

"And you're certainly not going to like new ones. I don't know why I wanted you to meet Elly and Marike. You're so predictable—"

"Unlike you, of course."

"I'm going back out to meet people and make the most of my first international travel experience. Would you rather come with me, or have some quiet time alone?"

Archer said nothing.

"I'll mention the bathroom door while I'm down there. Enjoy your quiet evening." Cane still in my hand, I turned around through the doorway and left him.

Scene Four

CHRIS REACHES HOME and hurries up the apartment steps to the keypad at the door. He punches in the number, feeling the Braille pad, and tells Devil, "Elevator."

On the ride up, Chris drums his fingers on the stiff leather harness handle, wondering what it's all about. Irritated by the whole morning but also worried for Trent.

He speed-walks along the hall to his apartment door, his dog keeping the harness tight. He finds the door, feels the sticker he has placed on the back of the knob to make sure it is his own, and turns his key in the lock.

"Trent? What happened?" Chris calls as he pushes open the door.

Devil starts in, then stops as suddenly as if he reached stairs.

Chris hesitates, listening, tension filling his muscles as the German shepherd sniffs beside him. Someone here who Devil does not know. Or something happened leaving a scent trail of enough interest to distract him.

Still gripping the harness handle, Chris starts to reach to feel the dog's face and follow the direction he is looking, when someone shouts.

"Surprise!"

Chris jumps back. Devil barks.

A dozen people call out, "Congratulations!"

Chris's heart hammers as he presses back into the door.

Devil barks again, but his tail is wagging, beating against Chris's leg, as someone hurries up to them.

"Congratulations, darling." Trent close before them, his hand resting on Chris's shoulder.

"What the hell's going on?" Chris whispers back.

Trent kisses him, though Chris is still recoiling. "Just a surprise party for you."

"A what? You called me from—? I was working, Trent. I had to leave a crime scene to be here."

"Oh." Trent hesitates. He strokes Devil's head. "I didn't realize that. You just said you had to go out, so I...rounded everyone up."

"Who? For what? It's not my birthday or—"

"To congratulate you for that case, silly. What'd you think? Your name's been all over the papers all week. We thought you deserved a little party." Now Trent is smiling, leaning in again, kissing his cheek. "Sorry, Chris. Don't be mad at us."

"Who do you have here?" He takes a deep breath. "I hate surprises. You know that."

"I don't think surprise parties are for the person who's being surprised, darling. They're for the people planning and doing the surprising. And I like surprises. So...tough luck." Trent tugs Chris's arm to draw him into the room, reengaging their friends.

Many people call congratulations, and men and women step forward to shake his hand.

"Thanks, Jamie. Hi, Ben." Chris shakes stiffly with them, still not recovered, awkward and disoriented with the attention and commotion.

"We've got shrimp cocktail," Trent says in his ear.

Chris jerks his head around sharply to the voice.

Trent laughs. "This is not *all* for me. And Michelle's homemade brownies."

Finally, Chris is almost smiling. "Okay...that...might be worth rushing off a crime scene for."

"Glad you think so. Congratulations, hero." Trent puts his arm around Chris's waist.

The party buzzes past in a quick blur of noise and motion and delicious finger food. The crowd quickly thins and the plates are emptied. No one lingering. More handshakes and hugs for Chris, then Trent sees the last guests out.

"Okay," he says, turning back to Chris, who is feeling around in the shrimp plate for stragglers. "We're alone. Do your worst."

"If you ever do that to me again, I will never come back home again."

"Whoa—okay. That's a bit worse than I thought your worst would be, but point taken. Anyway—" Trent's grin returns. "I don't have to do it again. Just one little surprise party for a job well done is enough, I guess."

"It better be."

Trent walks over and puts his arms around Chris. "Sorry you were working. I really didn't realize that part."

"But not sorry about the party?"

Trent laughs, pulling away, remaining with his hands resting on Chris's hips. "No. Not that part. But never more." Adding the last hastily as he leans in for a kiss.

"Okay." Chris sighs. "Thanks. I guess. For the...thought." He may hate surprises, but he loves Trent and it's tough to hold anything against him for long.

"Anytime."

Now Chris laughs, shaking his head as his phone beeps.

He pulls it from his pocket, tapping to get the voice-over to read back the new text. A message from Robert Perth.

Get down to the waterfront now. Ferry terminal. There's been another murder.

Chapter Sixteen

"OH, MY GOD, what a great story."

"So what happens next?"

They must have learned to talk like that from American TV. I found it easier and easier to forget I was even with Dutch people the more time I spent around Elly and Marike.

And I was, as it turned out, spending more time with them. After the altercation with Archer the night before, we only tentatively made up. He was still sulky, almost silent. I had told him I was sorry I'd snapped at him, but I wasn't sure what he wanted. He was letting his time there slip by.

Sulk and silence and huffing.

Then he did go out again today. I was glad to get rid of him. And, this time, not because I felt bad about him shuttling me around.

I had emailed the girls when he left, managed to write one more scene, and got a note back from Elly saying they would come by later in the afternoon.

I met them downstairs and showed them my work so far. It didn't take long to read the four scenes I'd put together.

They adored them. No critiques like Archer.

"You've got to say what happens next," Elly said. "You can't leave us wondering."

"I'm not sure." I took my laptop back, closing the screen. "I have all kinds of ideas and started scenes about what's going on. I'm just not sure which one will be the winner."

"Good luck. I can't wait to see it finished," Marike said.

"Are you alone for the evening?" Elly asked. "We're heading out to the coast. You should come."

"The coast? I don't want to completely ditch Archer."

"Why doesn't he come along?" Marike asked with a bit of a giggle behind it.

"He wouldn't, even if I asked. He's mad at me about me telling him he needs to get out more."

"Then you come along and let him stay in," Elly said.

After the way he was last night, that wasn't a bad idea.

Archer would be relieved to get back and find me still out for a while. Give himself time to stare at the wall or whatever it is he likes to do with all his required quiet time. He could shop for new furniture online or watch porn for all I cared, if that's what he needed to chill out.

"How do you get to the coast?" I asked.

They laughed. "We drive."

"Drive? You have a car here? You didn't take the train in?"

"Sure we drove here," Elly said. "I've got my car."

Archer certainly would grasp that I didn't mind being on my own, had my own independence, if I went out to visit the coast while he was walking around the city.

"How far is it?"

"Not far."

Vague, but hardly as if I had to do the driving.

It was soon settled. Talking about the fun we could have on a Friday night at the beach, the girls led me out after I returned my laptop to my room and grabbed my coat.

I had already climbed into the tiny-feeling car with them before I reached in my coat pocket and realized my phone was absent.

Damn. Disconcerting when you're making your break for independence. I couldn't just casually borrow anyone else's phone. First because of the interface. Second because of the foreign country. I wasn't even sure if anyone else's phone could reach Archer, having no idea about the overseas dialing.

But, oh well. It wasn't like I wanted to call him. I would come in late and show him I could have a perfectly good outing just like he could. He didn't have to be chained to me for the rest of his life. All grown-ups here. Well...maybe not these twenty-year-old college kids, but close enough. I was still in school myself so couldn't complain.

He wouldn't believe it when I told him I'd gone out of the city and got to check out the beach—not even taking my phone. Archer loves beaches. Which made me feel bad...

It was a stop-and-go slog to get out of the city. Elly and Marike laughed and chatted, slipping into Dutch now and then, reminding me that I really was in a new place. No descriptions either. I had no idea even what direction we were headed, only had a sense of leaving the city by the acceleration of the car—which felt like it would fly to pieces at any moment. I thought European cars were supposed to be sturdy. This thing felt like a tin can shot out of a cannon.

"There are so many great places," Elly was telling us. "You're going to love it. I've been out here before. Pubs, restaurants, shops, nightlife."

"Even this time of year?" I asked. "Won't it be cold on the beach?"

"We'll find out." She giggled.

The coast town she took us to was indeed livelier than I would have imagined.

The evening felt cool and dry, many people out, sun setting and I could feel the last edge of it through a clear sky. I loved sounds of the waves, relaxed by the soothing familiarity of it. I had always lived relatively near water.

What I found disconcerting was the lack of explanation. They had told me about the city and shops with enthusiasm. Now they were out to meet people and get drinks and dinner and walk on the beach.

I felt I had to offer to pay for dinner since they were driving and showing me around—sort of—but it almost exhausted the meager remainder of my cash. They explained to me that I didn't have to tip unless there was some extra special service received, but that made me squirm and I tipped anyway.

We ate fish and chips and all got a beer, them urging me to try the local stuff. It wasn't that I was a prude about beer. I'm happy to try local beers or whatever else. And I wasn't worried about them driving back. I guessed we'd be hanging out into the evening. But I hardly had the money for three beers in this place. The meal and drinks all together came to about eighty dollars US before a tip. We weren't even in the city now—this was the cheap food.

Feeling regretful that I could have taken Archer to a really special dinner in Seattle for that, or even a good one with just the two of us in Amsterdam, I followed them out to shops and surprising crowds.

"Isn't this off-season?" I asked, holding Marike's elbow and my cane as we slid through busy sidewalks.

"It's always tourist season around Amsterdam," Elly said.

Still no descriptions. I knew by the sounds that we were walking along a shopping area of a beachfront town. The sun was gone. Must be dark now besides shops and streetlights. But it wasn't that late because the sun was setting earlier and earlier now. I could hear waves only faintly to our right as we walked. But I knew Amsterdam had beaches north and west, so I wasn't sure if we were walking west or south because I didn't know which way we'd left the city.

I tried to ask about the town. They said things like, "It's really cute and old." Which is no help at all. There can be people and towns and cars and cats that are "really cute and old." Funny thing, but I'd been forgetting to appreciate Archer's rich use of details lately.

Wishing for Archer, wishing for my phone as I also began to wish I hadn't come out here, I felt somewhat comforted by a round of shopping in warm, noisy little places selling everything from coats and shoes to postcards and magazines.

They bought us local chocolate bars, which were so rich, I knew I had to get some for my mom. Wait and get Archer to find the same wrapper in the city tomorrow. I couldn't start carrying a shopping bag besides holding an arm and a cane.

"How about a swimsuit?" Elly said and both laughed.

It's hard to be in on the joke when no one tells you about the window displays you're walking past. Or maybe it was a person actually in a bathing suit that prompted the comment? Just no telling. And, more and more, it was sounding like there would be a lot I couldn't enjoy about this excursion.

Chapter Seventeen

WE FINALLY WALKED down to the beach itself: still people and voices around, waves now roaring.

Elly squealed, "Look at the fire! I told you there would be lots to do down here."

It turned out a bonfire had been built on the beach and a whole crowd of other young people, apparently on autumn university breaks, were out for a good time.

We started making friends and I felt a bit better to hear my companions eager to introduce me to their countrymen like a trophy: *Look at the cute, blind American we're showing around town. Aren't we special?*

I had to guess at the cute part since they gave their introductions in Dutch, but they would always keep to mostly English, either for my benefit or to show off in front of all present.

It would have driven Archer crazy. He's totally sensitive about prejudices of any kind. Doesn't matter if it's nationality or disability or race or origination or anything else. Doesn't matter if it's for or against, he doesn't like it. It would send him up the wall to think he was being pampered because he was American or gay or blind, rather than because he was Archer. He doesn't have many friends— always favoring the company of computers over people.

Anyway, I didn't mind being special. Far from minding, I loved how others made an effort in English for me and several people, male and female, shook my hand and asked how I liked Amsterdam. All looking at me when they talked. Not the pity stuff. Genuinely interested in the novelty of my being there.

I found a can pressed at me—"Try this, it's famous!"—heard the rising blaze along with waves, and felt sand below my shoes. New heat washed over me. I smelled pot smoke mixing with the wood fire.

Archer and I aren't into drugs. I have enough problems getting around sober and Archer's too stiff about everything. But I've smoked a few joints in my life, and it now crossed my mind that I had hardly smelled the stuff since we got there. Wasn't that supposed to be a stereotype? Yet I usually noticed more weed in Seattle than I did there.

I thanked the guy who gave me the can—more beer—then met a guy who told me he had dreamed of being a rock star in America since he was five years old—now going to school to become an engineer.

Another young man told me I looked like some bizarre name I could not pronounce or remember, though apparently a movie star from Amsterdam, so I assumed it was a compliment. Then a couple of young women asked if I wanted to feel their faces to see what they looked like because that's what they figured "you guys"—the visually impaired—do when we meet someone and they were totally fine with that if I did.

I'd never heard this about the Dutch, so I'm thinking it was the particular crowd I was hanging with and not a reflection on the country at all, but I felt like I was at a swingers joint. In the Age of Aquarius.

Maybe they were all just stoned? I could smell more of the stuff as the evening progressed. Or they just thought they were making a good impression by being friendly?

Conversations I could not understand buffeted me. Marike led me to a wood bench to sit, which surprised me because I was imagining we were way down the beach at a fire pit and far from things like benches.

She had a guy with her who she was laughing at as he chatted her up in Dutch. Or maybe he was telling her a funny story about hockey. I don't know.

"Mind if I ask…kind of where we are?" I asked at last as we sat. I pushed my beer can at her also. Way too bitter for me.

She took it. "We're on the beach." Still laughing.

"Fire is right in front of you," a male voice over my head and to the left—her amusing companion. "Don't walk into it."

"Thanks. I'd never have been able to feel or hear or smell it without the warning."

"You are welcome." All serious, thicker accent than Marike. "You wish you could see how pretty your girlfriend is."

Marike was laughing even more.

"I'm sure I would wish it if we were that sort of friends," I said. "I'll take your word for it, though. So what's behind us?"

"Rocks up the bank to the…to the…road and…shops."

"The town is behind us," Marike said. "The world is before us."

The man laughed. "Here, have this…"

"He cannot see, dummy." Marike went on for several more words in Dutch.

The man grabbed my hand off my own knee, no warning, and I jumped. Reek of weed as he bent over me, pressing a lit joint into my fingers.

"Thanks."

"*Geen probleem.* How do you come to the beach with beautiful from America?"

Wait...what? And Archer thought I got things messed up.

"They're not from America. I am." I pulled away, trying to push the joint back at him at the same time.

They both laughed at this as well. "Yes, yes. How do you come?"

"In their car."

"No, no, you keep that. We have much." Pushing my hand back at my chest. Then rapid words to Marike and they both walked off, her now chattering in Dutch.

Warmth off the fire was fantastic. I felt better knowing town and shops and people were just up the bank behind us.

When in Rome. So I tried a tiny, *tiny* hit of the joint.

I thought the top of my head was going to come off—like my feet pulled up through my body to collide with my brain, like I was thrown onto my ear in the sand. Jesus Christ. I didn't know what that stuff was, but it wasn't like the ticklish kind I'd tried at home. That had been like warm soup. This was like being slugged in the teeth with a living octopus.

I hated to just throw it away since, apparently, they liked the stuff. I also didn't know what I was throwing at. Maybe the fire was ahead, but not in my face.

"*Goedeavond. Hoe gaat het?*" A man plunked down on the bench beside me, once more making me jump.

"Sorry," I said, offering the joint to the voice. "Do you want this?"

"Thanks." He changed to English without missing a beat. "Do you know the blonde girl with the orange hat?"

"I'm afraid so."

"Does she have a boyfriend?"

"Do you know what the word 'subtlety' means?" I asked.

More laughing. "*Subtiel.* Better to ask and be direct than to walk into all kinds of...ah..."

"Trouble? Shit?"

"Misunderstandings," he finished.

"I guess so."

He clapped me on the shoulder. *Damn*, these people and their sudden moves. At least he took the joint with him when he left.

I remained on the bench—which should probably go without saying—and listened. Without anyone addressing me, however, I found no conversations in a language I could understand, though I'm pretty sure they were not restricted to Dutch. It sounded like French and something else was mixed in.

Cursing my own pass on getting a second language under my belt when I had the chance in school, I could only listen for tone and the waves and fire. The former were fading, tide clearly going out. The latter was growing all the time, pop and crack and ripple of the bonfire swelling in heat and energy. It was, in fact, becoming uncomfortable. I had to keep turning my face left and right and pull sleeves down over my hands to stop the heat from becoming too intense. I kept my cane in my hand all the time, so protecting my fingers was not easy. I couldn't risk losing the cane, already regretting being so blasé about my phone.

I waited ten minutes while the smoke smells—at least three kinds of smoke—and beer fumes and fire and conversation noise grew and grew. Cans popped, young men and women laughed endlessly. Someone very heavy slammed down into the bench next to me.

I leaped sideways and almost fell off. The bench had no back and no arm. Just a platform.

Giggling, panting breaths, muttered words I could not understand. Two persons. Male and female. By the sound of his voice, she had her hand in his pants.

In another moment, they were gone.

A high giggle far to my left and beyond the fire sounded like Elly. I should find her. This wasn't working out.

But another ten minutes passed and I didn't move.

I already felt like I had been waiting for an hour. Next time someone came past, I had to ask them about collecting Elly and Marike for me.

Archer might not have been surprised to return to the hostel before dinner and find me still gone with my friends, but he would be wondering by now. Still angry with me or not, I hoped he'd had a good day—hoped he was able to enjoy himself without me.

Which was really irritating to think because he obviously *did* enjoy himself without me, but he wouldn't admit it. Why? Why not just say he wanted to spend a couple days really taking in the city by himself in the middle of the trip?

Why did he pretend everything was fine while he was tense as a board and gasping for breath? Freaked out by the city and trying to protect me from it. It wasn't his fault Amsterdam was terrifying and we hadn't known in advance.

Every time he did something with me that he didn't really want to do, it was proof to him that he'd made a mistake. Proof to me that I'd been right. We never should have done this.

Which stopped me, made my blood run cold, despite the bonfire.

Did I really just think that? Did I mean it?

No, I was only afraid *he* thought it. Because he came on his dream trip and the only thing wrong was me. Looking after me. Taking care of me. He was twenty-four years old and newly married and condemned for the rest of his life to either travel like this or stay home.

Why had I gone through with it? I had known it was a mistake. I'd known it from the start. I'd certainly known when he proposed and I fled and told him no. How had he won?

He'd also known it was wrong. He had to. He'd known, but he'd done it anyway. It was insane.

Now I've been crushing him, blocking him, turning him into an old man with no prospects in his twenties. In a way, this served him right—being stuck with me. I had told him and told him and now look what happened.

But how to fix it?

What to say?

For every relationship there's a potential breakup. Only...it's not a breakup anymore. It's a divorce. Which is just as horrifying a thought as being alone on a beach in a foreign country with no phone and no Archer and no sight and nothing.

Which reached a full circle.

The noise was outrageous now. Music from somewhere, fire like a burning house. Smoke making me cough and choke, keeping my eyes shut so they were not burning and streaming as bad, skin painful with the heat.

Voices louder and louder, more and more. The classic college beach party, I supposed. Not that I had ever been to one. Smelling more than the beer and many smokes now. Other booze, fried meat, and something sweet being roasted in the fire. All the weed making them hungry. Someone probably brought a cooler of sausages and bags of marshmallows. Was toasting marshmallows a thing in Europe?

Had Elly known about this party? Had they both? Hooking up on Facebook maybe? All these people didn't just happen to stumble to this place in the dark. Or maybe it was an assumed school break thing?

In the dark.

I had to get up. Moving carefully, using the cane to step back around the bench, I turned my face from the heat.

I hit something, driftwood, sand, then something else. Someone's shoe.

A man said something to me in Dutch.

"Sorry. Do you know Elly and Marike?"

"Who?" He had to shout back in the din.

"Know anyone here called Elly or Marike?" I shouted. "Or see a blonde woman with an orange hat on?"

"Sorry." He was laughing—of course. "I can't see anything. Too much smoke." He went on chatting about the good time, still amused.

I tried to move farther from the gathering, but between the rough, rocky beach and chunks of driftwood, I wasn't making much progress.

I stopped again, turned back to noise, coughing and feeling the heat buffet me. They would see that I'd left my bench. They would come to find me. At least Marike would. She always seemed to be paying more attention. And we could get away.

Thinking more and more of Archer now, needing to get back to Archer, Archer not being here. Wondering if Archer was thinking this whole thing had been a mistake now. Not this trip. Us. Would he be able to admit the truth? That this was no life for him? That he could do a hell of a lot better than a blind guy for the rest of his days?

Any minute.

No one came over.

The mood seemed to be mellowing. Still a lot of shouting, a huge crowd. I couldn't imagine there were less than fifty voices out here now. Fire blazing, charred meat and chocolate filling the air with saltwater and all those smokes and human sweat.

They would notice. They would find me. Or...what?

I started back into the crowd, stopping people, apologizing, asking if anyone saw a blonde with an orange hat. The first two I tried did not speak more than a few words of English, adding a fresh flutter of fear in my chest.

The next two told me no. Finally, a young woman took pity on me and told me she would help me find her.

"What is her name?"

"Elly. Blonde hair, orange hat. And there's a dark-haired one, Marike. I don't have any idea what she has on besides a long coat, maybe a trench coat or peacoat."

"Let's look." She took my arm and I moved with her, cane in front, still having trouble on the beach. "What are you doing out here?"

"That's a damn good question," I said.

"Do you want a drink?"

"I just want to get back to my room."

"Where are you staying?"

"A hostel in Amsterdam."

"You came out here from Amsterdam? It's a long way."

"I noticed. If we don't find these people, I kind of...don't have a way back."

"There's a train. It will go into Amsterdam Central."

Great. But where the hell was the train station? And how would I get from Amsterdam Central to the hostel even if I had a train?

She looked. Nothing.

"Are you sure they're still here?" she asked.

That question stopped me, sent my fluttering stomach into a total belly flop. I felt sick. I needed Luath. I needed Archer. Hell, I needed anyone.

Chapter Eighteen

"HI, NOAH."

I jumped. Again. "Marike?"

"Are you having a good time? Who's your friend?"

God, I wanted to throttle her. Instead, I thanked my new aid profusely for offering to help and she happily left me with Marike.

"What's going on?" I asked. "Are you two all right? Can we get out of here?"

"Aren't you having fun?" She sounded surprised by my urgent questions. "Did you get something to eat?"

"I ate fish and chips back in the restaurant." I reached to find her arm. "Listen, I didn't bring my phone and I really should be getting back. Do you think we can find Elly?"

"Sure, she's right over here. But she's not ready to go yet." Giggling.

"Let me guess, she's met someone tall, blond, and handsome?"

"I would say so."

"Let's fetch her anyway and try to hurry things along. Please. I didn't know she meant to stay here all night."

"It's only twenty hundred."

Wasn't that 8:00 p.m.? I really had been sitting a long time, and waiting a long time.

"We've got to get out of here," I repeated.

Still laughing, she led me around the blaze and noise to find Elly.

Elly, though found, turned out just as reluctant as Marike had suspected. She said we'd just arrived and to enjoy myself. We'd leave soon enough.

Fighting a feeling of free fall, I didn't want to let go of Marike again, but she assured me she was ready to go at any time also and she would find me and we would all get out in another half hour.

My heart hammered as I released her arm for her to return to her babbling new friends. What was I going to do? I couldn't hang onto a near stranger who was trying to shake me. But I felt sick, stomach turning over, breathing through my sleeve to keep from choking on smoke.

I stood. I waited. I might have prayed a little bit.

Someone gave me another beer. I did drink a few mouthfuls, but my stomach flopped even worse and I was scared of throwing up on the sand, so I just held on to the plastic cup and the cane and waited.

It must have been well over an hour later, easy, me still on my feet, when Marike returned.

She grabbed my arm without a word, just blundering up to me.

I shied away, tripping back in sand.

"Need to get home," she muttered thickly in my face. I couldn't tell if she smelled especially like beer or like pot in the environment that already smashed me.

"Yes," I said emphatically. "Where the hell is Elly? Let's go."

Marike took our case to Elly and we badgered her until she agreed.

Still a long round of yammering with her new boyfriend in Dutch before she accompanied us away from the fire.

Fine. Okay. Deep breath. I might have irritated my hostess, but we were going.

"You two are party poopers," Elly told us from just behind and to the right as Marike led the way with me.

Marike lurched, perhaps holding her stomach with her free arm, seemed a bit bent over. She groaned softly, staggered, and stopped short on rocky, jagged ground that I could hardly walk over and was afraid at any moment of either falling or breaking my ankle.

I tried to step back as she vomited, caught a rock with my heel, and flew backward. Not my ankle that was hurt after all. I bashed my hip and scraped my palm, knocking the wind out of me and feeling more shaken and terrified of falling through nothing into sharp rocks than anything else. And my cane flew from my hand.

I scrambled after it, thinking more of that cane than my own pain or fear. Desperate for it. Lifesaving. After Archer, after Luath, I needed that cane.

Elly was laughing at us. Not a mean laugh. A stupid, drunk laugh and titter. Like we were just being silly.

There. My fingers closed on the thin, smooth plastic while my breathing came fast and my heart pounded.

Marike groaned.

I struggled upright, cane slick and damp in my hot hand.

"Where's the car?" I asked, but I wasn't sure I wanted it as we moved off again.

Marike still seemed to be suffering from midnight sickness and Elly, whose arm I was now attached to, could not walk a straight line. At first, I thought it was the rough ground, but the ground was not weaving around. It was just steep and rocky up the bank. Marike had been going straight.

Suddenly, my foot came down through air, pitching forward, then slamming into a gravel verge with my leading foot. Apparently, everything had leveled out. Thanks for the warning.

We struck out across pavement—the street they had mentioned, though there were no traffic sounds at this hour. Welcome sounds ahead finally of distant music, a distant car. Life and activity of homes or bars or hotels on the beach at night. Late people coming and going.

We were parked somewhere in that town, moving closer to the car, to getting in it. To driving.

"Elly," I started, "why don't you call Anna or your aunt? I'm not sure you should be driving."

"We already left early. Now you want me to have a babysitter also? I thought you were fun, Noah."

Yeah. I'd thought so too.

"There's such a thing as a limit," I said.

"I can drive," Marike offered feebly.

Elly snapped back something in Dutch, but the message was clear—hands off my car.

"How much did you have to drink, Elly?" I asked.

"Oh, my God! Lighten up. Do you want to get the train home?"

"Actually, it would be safer. If you don't want to call your aunt, maybe we should all get the train. Then we can take that tram line back to the hostel and you can come back tomorrow to get your car. Just leave it here for tonight."

"You really want the train?" She stopped on a sidewalk or road or something.

"Yes, I do. And you should too."

"Fine. Take the train." Abrupt turn, almost yanking me off my feet again.

I staggered. So did she, her center of gravity somewhere in orbit.

I wanted to tell her it was the smart thing, but I was losing popularity and didn't say anything. I was already worrying about how to pay for the train. Presumably for them as well since I was the one who had a bad attitude.

How much would it be? Was there a machine I could use my credit card at? Surely no one working in person at this hour in a tiny town.

Was the town tiny? I didn't even know its name.

We walked a long way, cold now, temperature plunged on a clear night and newly away from a blazing fire after all that time. I shivered even as we hurried along, though my companions seemed impervious to the cold.

"Here," Elly said at last while Marike gagged quietly behind us. "This is it."

"This is what?" I asked.

"The rail station." Words a little slurred, sounding like she had almost added, *What did you think, stupid?*

"Okay…"

She march-staggered on into…something. An echoing sound, surrounding walls. We passed through some sort of open structure and onto more concrete.

"Here's the platform and benches, right here." She turned and I tapped a metal, plastic-coated bench with my cane. She pulled her arm away.

"Where do we get tickets?" I asked, assuming that was what she headed for.

"It's right there." Tone more irritated with me.

She walked away, Marike's footsteps joining her after a few strides.

"I can get them," I said. "Do you know how much?" I reached in my zipped coat pocket for my wallet, fumbled with the zipper, pulled it out. "Elly?"

I listened. Footsteps faded into distant nothing. Not right-there steps. Walking-away steps. Back through the structure and down the sidewalk steps while I stood on the silent train platform in the middle of the night.

Alone.

Chapter Nineteen

I'D BEEN SCARED when I broke my finger in first grade playing backyard baseball. I'd been scared when I took my driving test. And when I found out I was going blind. And when the light really faded. Scared when I had to travel blind for the first time—going to the guide dog school in California to meet Luath. And scared with nerves on my recent wedding day.

So I'd thought.

That night, standing alone on a freezing, deathly silent concrete void, alone, I realized I had never previously been scared in my life.

I was so terrified, there were full minutes in which I could not think. I could not bring up a conscious anything. I could not move. I was not sure I even breathed. I felt like I was falling, being chased, drowning. I was so scared and so at a loss as to what to do next, I was starting to suffocate, to hyperventilate, maybe to faint.

Knees shaking, I hit the bench again with my cane, felt it, sat down. Still clutching the cane, I bent forward to put my head between my knees, mouth wide open, fighting for every breath, every second, as if struggling to remain alive.

Then I felt sick, like vomiting, like weeping. There were tears in my eyes with the sheer terror of what to do next— what I was facing, what was going to happen to me.

I have no idea how long I sat there. More than half an hour in the dead silence and the nothing—shaking, breathing, just panic.

At last I sat up, eyes shut, smells of all kinds of smoke still strong in my nose, thinking of Shiloh and Luath, of my mom and dad and, mostly, Archer.

What would I do if I had one of them here? They would help me. But what if they needed help? If I was out there with Archer and he broke his leg or had any kind of accident, I would have to get things done.

If Archer was around, he would want to figure out if, and when, there was a train. It was not *that* late. And a Friday night. There should be more trains, right?

There must be a display. There must be something telling about the schedule. Printed or electronic. I did hear the high, faint hum of electric something, but it could just be lights or the ticket machine or anything.

Next, assuming there was a train, get a ticket.

Right there.

There was a ticket machine nearby. Perhaps with Braille?

Forget the ticket machine. If a train showed up, or someone came to the platform, I could ask for help. Nearly everyone spoke English. There were people around somewhere. People in the town. People on the possible train.

Deep breath.

Okay.

People. I just needed people. Just one person to ask for help. Wait for people. The train would pull up and there would be people.

Simple.

If a train pulled up. If they ran late in these little towns.

What if the train did pull up, but I got on going the wrong way? What if I was thrown off at another stop because I had no ticket, then could not get another because that was the last train? What if the train just never came?

What would Archer do?

If he saw there was no train on the schedule, that we missed it, he would go back into town. We would stop in a bar or restaurant, or in a hotel or inn. We would ask for help and see if there was any other way to get into Amsterdam at this hour. Maybe the busses ran later. Or maybe we could get a taxi. That would cost a fortune, but it would be less than spending a night in a beachfront inn.

But Archer could see his way into town.

Still, we'd just walked through it. I had the cane. I could try. And what if I left the station and could not find the town with the bars and people to ask? What if I just started walking and found nothing at all? And could return to nothing?

More rippling panic, more short breath.

In, out. In through nose, out through mouth.

Then rumbling of a train.

Again, almost in tears, I stood up.

The grinding train was slow at pulling in. A hiss, then a faint whistle, scream sound. Closer, closer, coming in from my right.

I hardly felt the platform vibrate, hearing the noise grow and grow as I mentally prayed it stopped and people would appear.

There, pulling in. Close now, still moving slow, feeling the breeze of it pass some way before me. It stopped.

There was a great metallic sigh and huff and doors opened. I stepped up, reaching out with the cane, inching out on the platform, heart in my throat.

Then running footsteps, calling voices, young people shouting to one another in Dutch. People behind me, dashing in for the train, excited that they were not too late. Probably the last train of the night.

"Excuse me." I spun around. "Please. Can you help me get on the train? I'm trying to get to Amsterdam Central."

A confused rumbling met me and I realized in some alarm they were not Dutch at all. They were German.

"Amsterdam Central?" a young man said near me, voice thick with a harsh accent. "*Ja?*"

"Yes, *ja*, please. Amsterdam Central." Indicating the train. "Please, the door?"

"It is here," he said carefully. A large hand touched my arm.

"Thank you." Shaking, I stepped with the young guy and his friends to a door and up a step into the car at his prompting. "You're sure this goes to Amsterdam?"

"*Ja, ja*. It has a saying. It will say on…"

"On an intercom? Out loud in the train?"

"*Ja, ja*. Say out loud, Amsterdam Central."

"Thank you, thank you so much."

"*Viel Glück*." Then he and his buddies were gone, clambering away in the quiet train to go upstairs or downstairs or just find seats. I could only imagine.

Breath still burning, I stayed right where I was, feeling until I found a smooth, cold support pole to hang onto. I clutched this with my left hand, cane in my right, also checking with my right to make sure my wallet was still zipped in my pocket.

What about a ticket? What about being thrown off? Didn't anyone work on these trains?

The cane felt sticky, my right hand painful. I must have bled on it. I had forgotten about falling. The least of my troubles tonight.

Breathless, listening to every whisper of the rolling train, I waited, hoped, and thought of Archer.

I couldn't have been on more than five minutes when an intercom announcement did indeed come through the train in a scratchy, breathless way, as if the whole speaker system was on its way out.

Mhhhhmmrrrm mmmmr rrrrrem mmme rehhh.

Right. Obviously. Crystal clear. Just...one or two stops away. Of course.

Maybe the next one would come through more distinctly?

We had driven a while to get out here in the first place. The train would also take a while. And others would be getting off at Amsterdam Central. Just wait.

The train stopped. No one passed me, but a few people got on.

"Excuse me, please, do you speak English?" Still feeling like I was suffocating.

A quick muttering of Dutch, then someone stepped up close to me.

"Yes?" A woman. Not one of my young fellows, she sounded middle-aged or older, mature.

"Please, I've had...a bit of a mishap. I'm trying to get back to Amsterdam Central and I can't understand the announcements and I can't see the signs outside the train—or anything else. Am I even on the right train?"

"Your train is correct. There will be two more stops. One, two, then Amsterdam Central at the third."

I let out my breath. "Thank you so much. Thank you. That's a big help." Still feeling sick, I wanted to hug her, to hold on, ask if she would take me home.

"Are you American?" Unlike all the chipper young people so far this evening, she sounded concerned, close and a bit lower than my own face, looking at me while she spoke. This made me realize how tall most of the people around me had been in the past week. Not many adult voices in Amsterdam came from lower than my own face.

The train jolted onward with a lurch and picked up speed once more as I clutched the rail.

"Yes, that's right," I said. "I'm only here visiting Amsterdam and I'm blind. I wasn't supposed to be on my own. It was an accident."

"Do you have someone meeting you at the station?"

I shook my head, still resisting hugging her. "No, I need a taxi or...something. I'm staying by the park, Vondelpark."

"That's across the city."

Was it? I really had no sense of where Amsterdam Central was located. I had never looked at a map of Amsterdam in my life before losing my sight. Not that I would have remembered.

"Are there taxis at the station at night?" I asked.

"Do you have the address of where you are staying?"

"Yes." I fumbled for my wallet. "I have their card; Uptown Vondelpark Hostel."

"We must find a taxi for you at the station, and you show the driver your card, yes?"

"Yes, yes, thank you."

"Come sit down. Three stops away. Is your hand hurt?"

"It's nothing. I'm fine. I'll be fine. I just need to get back to...where I belong." *To Archer.*

"And do you have someone waiting for you at the hostel?" She pressed my arm, guiding me past another pole and into a fabric seat smelling of cigarette smoke and mustiness.

"Yes. I just need a taxi at the right place and I'll be fine. Thank you so much."

"Here, clean up your hands. Turn your palms up. I have hand sanitizer."

I did as she said, the cane now gripped between my knees as I sat and she sat across the aisle. I could not tell where her male companion might be who did not speak English and had brought her attention to me.

I gingerly rubbed my hands together when I felt the cold drops touch them, startled by the scorching pain where skin must be ripped off my right palm. The cane handle would be all bloody.

She passed me a tissue and I held that between my hands.

"You are having a hard vacation?" Sounded like a smile now, her voice gentle.

"You could say that. It was at least partly going well until tonight."

"Travel was invented to test us," she said.

Then I heard the man finally speaking again, behind her. He was at the window seat of the one she took across from mine.

They conversed for a moment in Dutch before she told me they would get off with me to help find the taxi. Again, I wanted to hug her, or just sob.

I did neither. I only kept thanking them all the way to the station and out through a nighttime crowd where she led me to a car along a busy sidewalk.

She spoke quickly in Dutch, I assume to the driver, and asked me for the address. I passed over the card. Another bit of conversation. Then she handed it back.

"Do you have a card?" I asked her. "Thank you so much." I felt my way into the seat and she passed me another stiff paper rectangle.

"That is me. Now you have a safe evening and take care of your hand. No more accidents."

"No. No more. Thank you. I can't thank you enough. Do you need a lift also? Where are you going?"

"Back for the next train." Another smile in her voice. "This is not our stop."

Then I really was near bursting into tears. So much more. So much worse. I could be dumped a thousand times and it wasn't as powerfully emotional as being treated like this.

"You didn't have to do this," I managed.

"It is nothing. It is all the same price." Her small, gentle hand rested on my shoulder, leaning in at the car door. "I have three boys, about your age and younger. If one of them needed help in a strange place, I want to think there is someone there for them to step off a train if needed. You just get home safe for me."

"I will. Thank you."

She squeezed my shoulder. "Good evening to you."

Then she was gone, closing my door, and the cab pulled away.

And I had no cash to pay for it.

Chapter Twenty

I DIDN'T WANT to explain to the driver until we got there that I could not pay him and would have to get into the hostel and see if I could find my husband for cash once we reached the place. I asked for the time instead—10:45 p.m.

About 11:00 p.m. by the time we arrived.

"Here you go," he soon called cheerily. "Front door steps are just out the left side of the car. Around a parked car. Okay?"

"Yes, thank you. I can get there." I was already opening the door, knowing my way around those particular steps. "I'll just run in and get you money. I'm sorry, I'm—"

"All paid."

"What?"

"The lady at the station paid for you. You're good. There's a man coming down the steps now. Looks like someone waiting for you?"

"Thank you—I—yes, thanks. Good night. Thank you."

I staggered from the cab and shut the door, getting my bearings with the cane to feel out the parked car as the taxi started away.

I had hardly touched the immobile vehicle with the cane when Archer's arms were around me, holding my back, grabbing my head and pulling me against him.

"What the fuck is your problem?" Archer's voice in my ear, breathless, his whole body shaking. "What were you—? Leave your phone, middle of the night—fuck, Noah. What was I supposed to do? No damn idea—Christ—"

I hung onto him, face against his shoulder, tears finally flowing, unable to speak at all, even to tell him I was sorry, though I tried, struggling to make my voice work.

Archer was apologizing, saying he was sorry while he held onto me and I couldn't think why he did but it made me feel a hell of a lot worse.

It took us a while to get upstairs to the room and bathroom. Though the party was going strong downstairs, it was again quiet for washing and cleaning up.

We pulled off our coats, and Archer helped me wash my hands and cleaned the cane for me. He didn't ask what happened, just using our own soap and telling me to turn my hands, then using paper towels.

"It'll be fine," he told me, speaking from inches away as he helped me bundle paper towels in place. "We have antibiotic cream with Band-Aids in the toiletry bag in the room. I'll put something on it. And you need to get those pants off."

Probably filthy.

I sat in my underwear and Pima cotton shirt on the bed while Archer dressed my hand, leaving the cane on the table to finish air-drying while fully extended.

"I'm sorry, Archer. I thought my phone was in my pocket and I didn't figure it out until I was in the car. It was just stupid. I didn't mean to worry you."

"You didn't worry me, Noah. You gave me ulcers. You took years off my life." He sat on the luggage bed, which we had sometimes pulled over to make one large bed, facing me. He held my hand with the cream and whatever little bandages he had sensibly thought to pack in a tiny, homemade first aid kit.

"I'm sorry," I repeated.

"Did you get dinner?"

"Yes. Did you?"

"Are you kidding? I haven't been able to eat anything all evening. You reek. Your coat smelled like a smokehouse."

"That's kind of what it was in. We went out to the beach. A bunch of college kids having a Friday night bonfire party out there."

"To the beach? You weren't even in the city?"

"Not in the city," I echoed. But I wasn't sure I could tell the story tonight. I just wanted to hold onto him.

"Did you have to use all your cash on that cab?" Archer pressed my hand back to me.

"No, I had to use it all on dinner and drinks. Can we brush our teeth? I just want to go to bed."

He rummaged and passed me my spare pair of pants to pull on so we could return to the hall bathrooms.

I tried to ask Archer if he wanted something to eat. He tried to ask me about the taxi.

We ended up in bed a short time later with unanswered questions on both sides.

"I'm really, really sorry I took off like that," I said, lying achingly back, careful with my right hand and right leg, freshly aware of my bruised hip. "It just sounded like fun to get out of the city and meet other people. It was stupid. I'm sorry."

"I'm sorry I wasn't with you, Noah. I'm just glad you're okay." He sat down beside me, leaned back to do something to the window, sliding it farther open or more shut. "And glad you're back."

"I'll tell you about what happened tomorrow. I'm just..."

"Fine. That's fine. It's almost midnight and tomorrow's our last full day here before we have to fly. We can't stay up all night."

Our last day? Was it really? I thought we had two more.

Both still shaking. He turned into me, arm around my back as I bent my painful knees and hunched down to press my head onto his chest. Again, I had a hard time not crying, so grateful to him for just letting us go to bed—work this out in the morning. Whatever all it was we had to work out.

Now, all I had to do was hold onto Archer and never let go. At least not until morning, which I never wanted to come.

Chapter Twenty-One

ARCHER BROUGHT ME oranges the next morning after I showered away the smoke reek that clung all over my skin and hair. Nothing to be done about my coat and clothes. We had washed clothes once on the stay. Now it was too late for more.

We ate bread, cheese, cold cuts, chocolate, a banana, and oranges for breakfast, sitting at the little table in the plastic chairs. Archer told me he had been to some landmarks and another museum, but he had really missed me. And that we needed to talk.

"I don't know why I let you talk me into going out on my own," he said as I tidied my orange peel mess onto the plate. "That was stupid. I should never have let you down like that."

"You didn't let me down. Don't be crazy. I told you to go. You should go. That wasn't the problem."

"But I shouldn't. I didn't want to."

"You did want to," I said. "You had a great time getting out and seeing things on your own. No babysitting and hand-holding and everything. This city is dangerous. You said so. It is. You needed a break. Don't pretend you weren't happy to get one."

"For a day. For one day, Noah. That was it. But you bullied me into going off again."

"I didn't bully you into anything."

"*You did.*" Raising his voice. "You do. All the time. I'm supposed to do and do, then I get my head bitten off and you tell me to take a hike. For what? I don't even know why you act like that."

"Like what?" I sat back in my chair. "Like I want you to have a life?"

"*We* have a life! Do you just not see that? Ever?"

"A life that needs more balance. You really think I'm going to be happy with you constantly throwing yourself under the bus for me?" I asked. "Is that what you want? Every single fucking day? Forever?"

"That's all I am to you? A caretaker? That's how you feel about this whole thing? Did you finally give in about the marriage thing because you thought that must be what I wanted? I only wanted to take care of you for the rest of your life because I'm some bleeding heart, but now you've got to set all the boundaries? Keep me away because you're perfectly independent enough to go off on your own and come back at midnight in a strange city every night of the week if that's what you want to do? Is that what the stunt was about yesterday?"

"It wasn't a stunt, Archer. You think I meant to come back alone?"

"I think you meant to put me in my place and prove you didn't need me."

I sat in silence, my ears ringing. I felt like he'd slapped me, so shocked, I couldn't think of a thing to say.

"I don't know what to do," Archer said in a quieter voice after a long pause. "I don't even know how to talk to you sometimes. Just when I think we're good, we understand each other, some dumb shit like this happens and I don't know...who you are. You obviously don't know me at all." He shifted or stacked things on the table and pushed back his chair. "The thing that gets me—that's just really infuriating with you—is that I don't think you want to work anything out. You want to make all the decisions. If they agree with what I want, that's great. If you've got to spit in my face to do what you want, then you're fine with that too."

Worse and worse, feeling like knives struck my guts, all the while his voice growing softer and slower. I had to swallow a couple times before I could answer him.

"I wanted to go out yesterday because you needed time on your own," I said. "Not me. Not what I wanted. You weren't even getting to see the city—"

"You don't listen to me, Noah. You never fucking listen." Voice even quieter. "For someone who really depends on listening, it's sad. I told you, spelled out to you, that I didn't want us to keep splitting up—"

"But you're saying it so I won't feel like I'm the albatross and baggage that I am. You won't say what you really want because you don't want to hurt my feelings. Of course you didn't let me down—it wasn't your fault. I just wanted to work on my comic book and meet people and have a good time. In a perfect world, you would have been there with me. We both could have gone to the beach or stayed in the city and seen some of the nightlife. But you hate that stuff and you needed space."

"You keep telling me what I want and think and feel, no matter how many times I tell you you're full of shit. If you were such a goddamn expert, we wouldn't be having this conversation." He stood up, grabbing the dishes from the table, and pulled open the door before I could say anything.

I waited in my chair while he presumably returned our dishes downstairs.

He would be gone a few minutes, but I wished it was longer as I had nothing but the hem of my shirt to attempt to dry my eyes with, struggling to breathe normally, not look like I was sitting there crying when he got back.

Five or ten minutes and Archer returned. He said nothing but began rummaging, pulling on his coat, shifting things.

"Archer," I started.

"Let's go out for a walk." He wasn't looking at me. I heard the zip of his jacket.

"Archer, just tell me what it is. Tell me where I'm wrong. I won't keep putting words in your mouth. I'm sorry if I've screwed up."

"Put your shoes on." He sounded tired. "I don't want to sit in here and talk on our last day. Let's go to the park."

I didn't want to go out. I didn't want the streets or park where we both had to think about what was happening around us. I just wanted to figure out what the problem was here and now.

But I got my shoes and coat on and followed Archer.

I shouldn't have let this happen. I'd known it from the start, of course. Not like it was me not wanting him. I would do anything for him. I had been devoted to Archer since the first day I saw him standing in the rain at our high school. My wanting him so much was the only reason I had caved and told him yes. That and prompting from Shiloh. I knew I didn't deserve him. Now, I realized I had been right all along. Because Archer clearly didn't think I deserved him either.

I made my careful way out to the street after him, and Archer stood while I found his elbow. He told me the way in a monotone and I shivered and tried to stay close.

There was a fine autumn breeze in the air, damp but not quite raining. People out in the park this morning, bike bells, dog tags, parents calling to children. Saturday morning, I realized. The place was bustling. Another reason we shouldn't be out.

We walked on a dirt path or road, my dark glasses on, head bowed anyway, just trying to hear Archer's breathing, his voice, his heartbeat. Instead hearing nothing but his footfalls and his silence in a loud world.

"I'm sorry you think I'm never listening to you," I said after a long time of our silent walking.

Archer sighed. "There you go again."

"Go with what?"

"You're sorry 'I think' you don't listen. That's not the same thing as a real apology, Noah."

"Okay. I'm sorry I don't listen to you."

"Thank you," he said softly.

Nothing more.

"What is it I do?" I asked. "What am I saying that you're saying or thinking when you're not?"

He snorted. "Where to start? You're always putting words in my mouth. You think you know everything. That's why, when I try to tell you about my side of things, you just roll your eyes or laugh or think, 'Poor Archer. He obviously doesn't know what he wants or what is good for him. I'll make the choices for him, then he'll see how much happier he can be with a little outside help.'"

"That's not even—" I felt angry again, trying to stop him, but he rushed on.

"For example, pushing me for a relationship when all I needed was someone to talk to."

Yes, Archer had mentioned before that I was way too pushy in high school—that was before I went blind. He had been grieving and newly moved, yet I was kind of all over him. Only once I backed off did he become comfortable.

"Then," Archer said, "you wouldn't move in because you didn't want to put me out. I had to bend over backward just to show you it was okay when all you had to do in the first place was say yes. After that, I put myself out there and proposed, and you walked away from me with your dog on a beach and told me to go to hell."

"I never said that to you—"

"You said it with your back, Noah."

"Because I didn't want you to be stuck—"

"You're still not fucking listening to me!" He stopped abruptly to face me. I let go of his arm. "You say that over and over. You did this and that and the other 'for me.' It's all for me. But it's not. It's for *you*, Noah. Until you can admit that, I don't know where this is going. I don't know what we have. I thought you'd dealt with your insecurities or relationship sabotage or whatever and we were going to be okay when you came back and said yes, but I just...don't know now.

"It feels like every few minutes you walk away and turn your back and do what you want because you're scared. You're scared that you're going to say yes and then you're going to be comfortable and happy and I'm going to burn out and leave you. You've been scared of being dumped ever since you went blind. You didn't have an insecure bone in your body until then. You even had a good school and a cool family and an artist mother. Everyone was into your art and didn't care that you were gay. You were the fun, pretty boy, not so extreme in any direction that you even ever had peer problems or grade problems or anything problems. Even when your parents split up, it was amicable compared to some families. Everyone still rolled along. You didn't know what it was like to be really, really alone in the world. You didn't know what it was like to be scared of rejection. You didn't know what it was like to be so terrified of failure, of losing everything you loved, that you suffered from night terrors for *years*. Then you went blind and, for the first time in your life, you thought you might be unlovable—that you could lose everyone. That opening yourself up could be dangerous. So, yeah, for the first time in your life, you did go from boundary issues to intimacy issues.

"But the really fucked-up part, the sick, twisted part is that you already had everyone in place. You had your mom watching out for you. You had your dad, who you could call if you needed to. You had a great sister who didn't mind helping you get around. You had me finally allowed to take a deep breath and come to you myself instead of being badgered by you. Then you even had the dog and friends and coworkers and people you could call at the resources boards. I'm not saying it's not crap to have a disability of any kind. I'm not saying you wouldn't change it if you could. I'm not saying it's not a fucked-up thing to begin with. But your 'disability' opened new doors for you and gave you a whole new community and group of people to embrace and support you. While I still had only a mom and grandparents who I was afraid I could lose by coming out—plus you. That was it. Period."

Archer was breathing hard, talking very fast. "Then, you made your next awesome decision to 'benefit others.' You said no to me. That was everything to me. Terrifying to me. Because I was scared of rejection and scared of being gay and scared of losing my family and scared of publicly marrying a man. And I asked. Because I loved you so much, it was worth the risk. And you walked away because *you* were scared too. Yet you still don't think I get that? No. You have the nerve to keep telling me your choices are 'for me.' You don't want me to be saddled with you and take care of you. You don't want me to be put out. You don't want me to be inconvenienced. You're a liar, Noah. Maybe you feel like that some, maybe it bothers you that you feel like I'm too committed to watching out for you. But you walked away and hid and sulked and took months to come back to me for exactly the same reasons you have been on this trip—because you're afraid of being rejected. You're afraid that I'm going to push you away. Either for an hour or a day or a lifetime. That I'm going to say 'Back off, I've had enough. This is too much work for me.' Either for right now or forever.

"And while you're busy being scared of losing me, you are pushing me away. And you're driving me insane. I can't keep this up. You can't keep pretending it's all about me when it's all about *you* and you won't even look in an emotional mirror and admit you've got a problem.

"Do you know how many people have been insecure in their lives or feared rejection or feared losing someone they love? Pretty much everyone. Everyone who loves someone. Everyone who has friends and family. Everyone who has ever been in a romantic relationship.

"I enjoyed one day out. I saw a lot of stuff. It's been incredible seeing this city. But one day was enough. I wanted to spend the time before, and the time after, with you. I wasn't pretending. I wasn't 'sacrificing' to be with you. I really, really wanted to be with you. And you skipped out on me and terrified me and made me wonder for the first time ever if this wasn't a really big mistake and there was nothing I could do to hang onto you, no matter how hard I tried. Do you know what that's called without any word confusion? It's a self-fulfilling prophecy. Also known as digging your own grave."

Archer finally stopped. And, though he had been talking for minutes and I should have had time to think, I still found I could call up nothing to say.

Chapter Twenty-Two

I WENT ON being silent for so long, I guess I worried Archer because he finally asked if I didn't have anything nasty about him to counter with.

But there isn't anything really nasty about Archer. There never has and never will be. That's why it was so crushing to realize I'd let him down so badly. That all the shit we'd both been going through was my fault and I could have just talked to him at any time. But, before all that happened in the last couple days, I might not have listened.

"Come on," he said softly after a bit, and we started walking again.

The forward momentum seemed to unstick my tongue, yet all I could start with was "I'm sorry, Archer."

Archer sighed. "I don't want you to be sorry. I want you to think about what you're doing and not make decisions for both of us."

"I don't want to lose you. I don't know—"

"Then start acting like it. Instead of pushing me away. Because I know that. I get it. I get insecurities. I really, really do. Maybe better than anyone you know. But I've also faced them. I catch myself. I ask myself, am I doing this for me? Or for my own fear? Am I doing what feels good and what I want and hope they will accept, or what I *think* they want and am desperate for them to accept?"

As it turned out, Archer's mom and grandparents had managed okay about him being gay. Not happy. Not even blasé about it. But they were working on it. They still loved him, still tried to support him.

I closed my eyes and bowed my head as we walked.

I couldn't get all sniffly about this, or I would only look like I was feeling sorrier for myself for him chewing me out. Though I wasn't thinking about myself. I was thinking about Archer watching me walk away from him with Luath that day on the beach at sunset when he'd risked everything and I told him to go to hell. And he was still around. Still giving me another chance. Still forgiving me.

Archer went on walking in silence but put his arm around my back, and I leaned my head into his shoulder. I took a deep breath.

"I'm really sorry," I said again and swallowed.

I smelled earth and smoke and Archer. I heard bikes and feet and Dutch voices and a dog bark. Mostly, I felt and heard Archer beside me. At least, now I tried to hear him.

After a while, I started to explain about the outing—what led to my going to the beach and leaving my phone.

"Why didn't you borrow someone else's to call me?"

"With the international calling, it never crossed my mind once I was out there. But there wasn't much chance. By the time I was with someone who would have offered a phone, they were sending me home."

Archer didn't say anything else while I told him about the party and my refusal to get in the car with Elly driving, which led me to being abandoned at a deserted small train station alone at night.

I told him about the Germans who had said I was on the right train, then my guardian angel, who'd put me on the taxi.

I stopped on the trail to reach in my pocket for my wallet and the business card.

Archer chuckled when he took the card. "I'm not going to try to pronounce the name for you. Aleida something. I can't tell you what she does either. Uh...*hoogleraar*? It looks academic. I think it's a school card? Some kind of teacher."

I smiled. "I came full circle? From the students to the principal's office?"

"You were really lucky, Noah."

"Yeah." He gave me back the card, and I took his arm again. "I am."

"There's an email address. We'll tell her thank you."

"Please. I would like that."

"Noah—"

"I know. I have no intention of ever doing anything like that again. Not in any country. Not with anyone I don't already know and have reason to trust."

He let out a breath.

"I'm so sorry I scared you, Archer. At least I knew what was happening. It must have been awful for you too."

"It was one of the worst feelings I've ever had," he said softly.

I thought of his father being shot and killed, his mother having to move him to Olympia to live with his grandparents, him having to come out to his family, his proposal and me walking away.

"I'm sorry," I whispered.

He took my hand to slide down his arm, so he was holding my left with his right. "I'm just glad you're okay."

Was he still questioning us?

Was I?

I pressed his hand in mine, taking a deep breath as we walked.

"Archer? Is it too soon to ask if we can start over?"

"Never too soon to ask."

"Maybe just to start."

"What we're doing hasn't been working well so far, Noah. I'm not sure...we know how to start over yet."

"We'll never know until we try," I said.

"Yeah..."

"What do you want from me? What do you need from me most?" I asked.

"I need you to face your own issues and not make them mine. I want you to accept that I love you and want to be with you. And get that your not being able to see is really not as big a deal to anyone around you as it is to you. Mostly, I need you to listen to me. Really listen and respect what I'm saying."

"Okay. Then that's what I'm going to do."

"And what do you want?" he asked.

"I want you to set boundaries so I know and don't have to guess. If you never stop yourself, I'll have to make up times I feel like you need a break. You have to tell me. You did need and want one day and you wouldn't admit it. Because you just give and give. Which you noted. I need to know that, when you want a break, you will say, 'I need a day to do something on my own.' Or however long. For whatever reason. If I know you'll say when you have something important, I won't try to make them up for you."

"All right. I'll do that. But you can't lose faith in me at every bump. Okay? You have to know that my spending a couple days with my family or going to a movie with friends because you're not much for movie theaters these days, doesn't say anything about you."

"I know. I won't lose faith in you. I have a comic outline to work on these days. And I'm supposed to be finishing school, then advancing my career."

"I'm not worried about your career. I don't care what you do as long as you're doing *something*. I just care about us. Us being okay."

"I know."

We walked for what must have been a couple of miles, all the way around the giant park in the heart of the crazy canal city.

We stopped again on the little arched bridge, now in blazing autumn sun. And now, I knew, with other people around, and Archer kissed me. I didn't know what I did to deserve him, but I decided I wasn't going to ask anymore. I was going to enjoy every moment.

Chapter Twenty-Three

AFTER DINNER, ARCHER started packing and planning. I wrote to thank my angel, with his help.

I was just about to send it, when I asked Archer if he heard someone knocking.

He did not. He never did hear anything.

"It's been going on for a while. You don't hear that?"

"They told me they fixed the door," Archer said.

"Right." I got up from the table.

We went down together. Sure enough, pounding and occasionally calling through the door.

A young woman. "Help! Anyone out there? The door won't open. Hello?"

"An American?" I asked Archer.

"Sure sounds like it." He opened the door.

"Oh." I could hear her jump back, panting. "Thank you. Thank you so much!"

"No problem." Archer was smiling. "You're not the first."

"What? Why don't they fix it?"

"Ask them."

I chuckled. "Have you tried the chocolate on white bread?"

"That's my favorite." Smiling then. "I can't believe we don't eat that at home."

"Where are you from?" I asked as we all started back down the hall and around the L-turn.

"Portland—Oregon, not Maine."

"No shit. We're in Seattle," I said. "Heading back tomorrow."

"Any tips? I just got here with girlfriends and was so jet-lagged I couldn't go out to dinner."

"Most important: if anyone invites you to the beach, don't go."

"What?"

"Come hang out with us while you're waiting for your friends to get back if you want to," I said. "We're just packing up. Noah, and this is Archer."

"Thanks. That's a sick name. I'm Olivia."

She was happy to share the cheese and bread we'd stocked in for our trip the following day. I told her to check out the park across the street. Archer told her the two best museums and to get there very, very early to wait in line at the Anne Frank House. I told her about the best hole-in-the-wall easy-to-miss fry place, and Archer gave her our paper map from the hostel where he had been marking such things.

She told us how excited she was to be in this awesome city and how she couldn't wait to see all this stuff—but mostly try the fries.

Even Archer laughed.

Her people soon came to find her, and we said good night and exchanged emails.

Archer was still chuckling when the three girls left us.

Closing our door, he put his arm around me and kissed me.

"You know, Noah, I'm sorry about your boundary issues, but I kind of like it sometimes."

"You just wouldn't talk to anyone if I wasn't here, would you?"

"No, actually, I wouldn't."

"And look at what we would miss. The good, the bad, everything. You wouldn't meet any Ellys, but you wouldn't meet any Aleidas or Olivias either."

"But you wouldn't need Aleidas in your life without the Ellys, would you?"

I slid both hands up along his face, holding him, kissing him. "Maybe it's worth it. Maybe we would never find the best in one another without the worst. Maybe we would never appreciate what we had without being shown what we have at stake—what we could lose. I'm glad I met Elly and Marike. I wouldn't be standing here with you, like this, starting over, if I hadn't."

"You're impossible, Pollyanna."

"Isn't that why you love me?"

"Maybe. Just a bit."

He was still planning as we went to bed, telling me the number of the shuttle we had to get back to the station, wondering if we should get a cab since we had the rolling bag to deal with now as well.

I laughed at him. "It doesn't matter, Archer. We don't have to rush out at the crack of dawn. We'll be fine, however we go. I'm not worried about it. We'll do it together. Though mostly you, of course."

Then Archer also laughed, telling me he didn't mind—at least we understood each other.

I pulled off his shirt, kissed his chest instead of his neck, felt his arms, his back, his face, kissing his lips, imagining his blue eyes.

"Happy honeymoon," I murmured.

"Happy honeymoon, Noah. It's been…"

"Memorable?"

"Definitely memorable."

Scene Five

YELLOW CAUTION TAPE sags in the renewed afternoon rain. Blue and red lights flash. Crowds of people stand back on sidewalks and footbridges, murmuring to one another, making phone calls, or trying to snap a picture. Both the Bainbridge Island and Bremerton ferries sit out in Puget Sound, not permitted to pull in and disgorge passengers until granted police clearance. US Coast Guard boats zip through the harbor. Rain falls on a dozen cops and investigators swarming the outer terminal like gnats.

And there. Dr. Chamaeleo lifts his own phone in his right hand, zooms the screen in, and finds a slim man in a black overcoat, black glasses, and with a black dog at his side. The dog wears a heavy leather harness, pulling the man along at a brisk pace as they reach the top of steps. They are allowed past the police tape and start toward the head of the terminal.

One, two, three photos Dr. Chamaeleo snaps. He leans back into the railing of the footbridge he shares with dozens of others, crowding onto it from Seattle's 1st Avenue. One nice, clear shot, a side view of man and dog before they bowed under the tape that a cop was lifting for them.

Dr. Chamaeleo taps the screen to open an email with the photo displayed.

Whiteout—this the man you're looking for? 100 yards from me right now. Anything you want with him?

He sends the message and lowers the phone to watch the proceedings on the dripping terminal. The blind man now seems to be having a discussion—an argument?—with a couple of the cops.

What might he gain by this association? Getting on Whiteout's good side? The idea of Whiteout being in his debt makes Dr. Chamaeleo shiver with pleasure. Anything he can do to lend a hand...

His phone vibrates. Dr. Chamaeleo checks the screen.

I want him crossed out.

Oh. That bad, was he? Well...all the more indebted for the scale of the job. All the better.

Dr. Chamaeleo pockets his phone and slips from the crowd.

Chapter Twenty-Four

"YOU KNOW...I don't understand why you're so bent on writing a comic book," Archer said in the noisy airport as he pushed my laptop back at me.

I took it, shifting to face him in the vinyl seat as we sat side by side.

What? Now this was going too far. I tried to bounce back from his criticism, but that I should give it up?

I closed the laptop, feeding it back into the sleeve, starting to ask what that was supposed to mean—was it really so bad?—but Archer sat up beside me.

"There's our boarding announcement."

"You know this is just starting," I told him. "Just rough." I tried to put my bag back together while Archer stood and adjusted his own backpack beside me.

"Have your ticket ready?"

"Oh, God, they just made the announcement, Archer. The plane isn't going to leave for forty-five minutes. Chill. You really think it's that sucky?"

"No. Stop being so judgmental about everything I say. Your outline's not bad. You've got a great idea. It could be a great story."

"Then what's wrong?" I zipped my bag and stood up, heaving on the backpack. "Have your toothbrush with you?"

"Yes, I do," he said. "But we're going home this time."

"You never know." I chuckled.

"Don't say that, Noah. You've got a really lousy sense of humor sometimes."

"Unlike you? Anyway, sometimes is better than all the time. I'm going to miss this cash system," I added as I pulled my paper ticket from my inside jacket pocket. "I don't know why dollars are so backward."

"Laziness? What are you doing with that card?"

"What card?"

"You've got a...paper flyer for something. Did you pick it up in the train station?"

"This is my boarding pass." I held it up.

"No, it's not."

I caught my breath. "What? You just gave it to me an hour ago when we checked in. You're the one who—" I felt it with both hands. "It is, Archer. This is what you gave me."

He was laughing, walking away from me.

I cursed him so much as I grabbed my cane from the seats that Archer told me there were children present and to shut up.

"Why are you so horrible to me?" I asked under my breath as we stood together, waiting in line.

We could have had priority boarding. We just never bothered.

"Why are you so horrible to me?" Archer shot back.

"I'm *not*. You don't know what it's like."

"Why don't you run off with someone else to look out for you who's more fun?" Archer asked. "There's a good-looking guy up ahead. He probably has a better sense of humor and loves to go to beach parties. Go ahead. Ticket ready," he prompted me.

We passed the gate agents with their scanners, then waited for much longer inside the ramp down to the plane itself. I didn't like the empty feeling below my feet. Or the cold. Or the weird, hollow, mechanical and human noise. I mostly didn't like that Archer had distracted me from the matter at hand.

"So you're serious? You think I should just give up comic books before I waste any more time?"

"Is that what I said?" Archer sighed.

"Yes."

"What did I say?"

"You said I shouldn't be doing a comic."

"There you go. I know you love comic books and that was always your thing, but you're holding onto a visual medium that is going to lead you to a lot of frustration if you really go for it. If that's what you want, you should do it. Whether it's just for fun or you want to pursue publishing or work with an artist and publish yourself—or whatever. If that's really what you want. But is it? Because I wonder if you're approaching this the wrong way."

"How would you approach it?"

We kept walking forward periodically, foot by foot, and Archer held my arm so I wouldn't walk into anyone or whack small children with my cane.

"Why do you want the artwork involved? If it was me, I'd want to try something on my own. I'd want to get something done for myself first. Then maybe think about doing a comic."

"Meaning?"

"A book, Noah. Why don't you write a novel instead of a comic? Take the idea, take the characters, and write a gay blind superhero novel and see where that gets you first. That's all yours. No artist. No stress for you having to figure out that side of things. I know you can write a novel if you can just sit still for long enough."

"I don't know... Novels are long."

"So are comic outlines. You're a reading maniac. Don't you think you could write a novel? I mean, your outline is sounding more and more like one already, the way you're writing it."

I didn't say anything. But…maybe I could.

"I'll help you with it. I know that software does dumb-ass things with the voice-to-text sometimes. I'll brush up on my grammar. And Shiloh would love to read something like that if you don't mind her seeing it. She'd give honest feedback. But—" Noise louder now, and much colder, close to stepping into the plane itself. "Can you finish a first draft before you keep pushing it at me? You need to have a clear idea in your own head before you ask the rest of the world."

"Yeah, I know. Go ahead of me. I don't like you pushing me down the aisle."

"Yes…" Another sigh. "I've noticed."

I held his shoulder and kept close against his backpack as he led the way through the crowded, tight aisle down to our cheap seats in the back of the plane where we were hoping for another row of three to ourselves.

This time, we ran out of luck.

A Dutch guy showed up while we were still getting settled and Archer turned the window seat over to him so he didn't have to sit between us for twelve hours. He was much obliged.

I wished we'd gotten seats closer to the front of the plane and less noisy if we were going to have to share. But half of our air travel had been spacious anyway. Can't win them all, I guess.

I sat in the middle, Archer on the aisle. Pulling off my coat as we all settled and rearranged, I felt through my zipper pockets, which had served me faithfully throughout the trip. Funny, I was sure my passport was in my inside pocket with my boarding pass, in case they wanted it at the gate like they had at security.

"Archer?"

"Do you want your coat up in the overhead?"

"I can't find my passport."

"Very funny, Noah. Do you want it up or—?"

"I mean it. I can't find it. It should be in my pocket."

"Are you serious?"

"I'm damn serious. It's gone. I had it at security and they looked at it and then I put it in my pocket with my ticket...I thought."

"You must have put it in your bag. I'll look."

I felt again through every pocket while Archer searched my bag.

"Anything?" I asked him.

"No." He checked the coat also. "Crap, Noah. Where is it?"

"In the Amsterdam airport somewhere? But we're just going home now, so—"

"Just going home? We kind of need it for reentry."

"We do?" Wasn't thinking about that.

"Yeah, you do. They don't just take your word for it that you're an American citizen." He searched his own pockets, opened his bag, and pulled stuff back down from the overhead. "Dammit, Noah. I'll go back through the plane and check at the gate." He stepped out into the aisle and threw stuff back overhead. "It looks like they're done boarding—shit."

"Hurry."

"There's someone I can tell about it—"

He started away and a female voice called from the front of the plane, "Noah Pearce?"

I stood up, ramming my head into the overhead... whatever, light and call button and vent and all the shit that's up there under the overhead bins. I cursed again, grabbing my head and the seat back against my chest.

Our Dutch neighbor in the window must have been enjoying the show.

I scrambled out into the aisle. "Do you have it?" I asked stupidly.

"Over here." Archer let out a breath as he moved back against me in the aisle so the flight attendant or gate agent, or whoever, could reach me.

"You are Noah Pearce?" Was she comparing the photo?

"Yes. Seattle. US passport." I held out my hand, even starting to rattle off my birth date, but I think she believed me from the picture.

"There you go." She pressed the stiff passport into my fingers. "Enjoy your trip."

Archer thanked her and asked where she found it—it had been turned in at the gate while we were boarding—then we resettled in our seats.

"You really know how to get the most out of travel," Archer said a short time later as the safety videos started and the plane backed from the gate. "If my cardiovascular highs are any indication."

"I've heard that getting your heart rate up on a regular basis is good exercise."

"Exercise that gets your heart rate up can be good. Not just having the heart palpitations randomly. Don't ever quote this stuff at people, Noah." He sighed.

"I'm really glad we came. I mean, maybe you don't believe me—"

"No, I believe you. I'm glad we came also."

"What are we doing for our next honeymoon? After I've got my breakout novel done? Somewhere simple? Moscow? Tokyo?"

"Next honeymoon?" Archer asked. "Who are you planning to marry next?"

"You don't have to get married again to have another. It happens every year."

"You're talking about the *anniversary*, not the honeymoon."

"No, the honeymoon," I insisted. "People do anything for an anniversary. The honeymoon is a trip away with just the two of us. Every October. Every year's a honeymoon."

"Where do you get these ideas?"

"I'm just smart, I guess. You know what's in San Francisco in October?"

"The film festival?"

"That too. No, the Castro Street Fair."

"Uh-huh."

"We can get tickets to San Francisco for less than two hundred each. Stay cheap again, have fun."

"Uh-huh."

"You don't want to go to the Castro Street Fair?" I asked.

"Well, you know I'm *usually* into stuff like street fairs and pride parades and carnivals and cross-dressing. But, just this one time, I don't know..."

"You know what I think you're into? I think you're into Golden Gate Park. The Japanese Tea Garden. The California Academy of Sciences. Miles of beaches. The history in The Haight and Mission Districts. Museums and used bookstores. Walking along the waterfront in the sunshine and trying fresh seafood. Visiting Alcatraz."

This seemed to have gotten his attention because he paused.

"Maybe." Now, I could just hear his smile as we sat very close, faces near each other to be heard in the noisy craft.

"And I'm into the Castro Street Fair," I added.

"And I'm into you," Archer said.

"So, maybe...we can work out a compromise for the next honeymoon. No passports. No twelve-hour flights. Two hours and a few clicks with a credit card. But we do still get to travel. Still get to check something off your list."

"They say that's what lasting relationships are all about, don't they?"

"Compromise?"

"Yeah."

"They are full of shit," I said. "Lasting relationships are about communication. That's what I've learned on this honeymoon. Real relationships are about honesty and commitment. And about...friendship just as much as love."

"What will we learn on the next one?"

"We'll learn that everything gets better with time."

"You are so sappy, Noah. And fun and crazy and... different. Like this city. I can't wait to read your novel."

"I can't wait to write it. And you to make it better for me. Because you always do. Make everything better, I mean."

"Now you're going to gag me with the saccharine stuff. Should we have another wedding cake next year also?"

"Why not?"

"Chocolate espresso this time."

"You wanted the citrus cake," I said.

"No, you wanted the citrus cake. I just humored you. But, this honeymoon is over, right? I'm supposed to be assertive now, put my foot down and set rules and stuff."

"Not about cake, Archer. Only about your personal boundaries and needs and limits. Who wants a coffee wedding cake?"

"Who wants a lemon one? That's an old lady cake."

"Your mom loved it."

Another sigh.

"I can't wait to get back to Luath and start my novel and settle in as a married man."

"Me too. Besides the novel. You work on that."

"It was a hell of a lot easier getting around check-in and security and a packed airport and the gate and plane than it was to get around Amsterdam. Did you notice?"

"Amen, brother," Archer muttered.

The plane finished taxiing and turned. The engines roared; we surged forward.

"I love you, Archer."

"Love you too. It's been amazing, seeing this place with you."

"Very funny," I called in his ear, pressed back in my seat. "This was the best honeymoon I've ever had. I can't wait for the next one."

Archer laughed.

"With you, I mean, of course. You know that. Not like a new-marriage honeymoon."

"I know what you mean. This time." He was still chuckling as we took off, heading home.

Acknowledgements

With thanks to Michael and David for sharing your home so near both the Rijksmuseum and the best fries in Amsterdam. To Leigh and Vasco, my fellow Amsterdam explorers. And to the NaNoWriMo community; this story is also your story. Thank you all.

About the Author

Jordan Taylor is the author of numerous works of fiction from epics to short stories and poetry, with novels including co-written *Witches of London* titles with Aleksandr Voinov. An avid reader and writer, Jordan is also an obsessive photographer, lover of travel and ice cream, and one of those people on social media who posts too many cat pictures.

Instagram and Twitter: @JordanTaylorLit

Website: www.jordantaylorbooks.com

Other books by this author

Guardian

The Places We Say Goodbye

Also Available from NineStar Press

Connect with NineStar Press

Website: NineStarPress.com

Facebook: NineStarPress

Facebook Reader Group: NineStarNiche

Twitter: @ninestarpress

Tumblr: NineStarPress

www.ingramcontent.com/pod-product-compliance
Lightning Source LLC
Chambersburg PA
CBHW060548190726
48283CB00003B/926